# THE GIRL WITH A PORCELAIN FACE

## A GHOST STORY
### BY
### STEVE MCELHENNY

First published in 2023 by:
Sicaso Publishing Ltd of Piccadilly Business Centre, Aldow
Enterprise Park, Manchester, M12 6AE.
www.sicasopublishing.co.uk

All enquiries should be addressed to
sicasopublishing@gmail.com
ISBN 978-1-3999-4862-3
Cover designed by Sicaso Publishing Ltd

# DEDICATION

This book is dedicated to the loving memory of my dad, David 'Mac' McElhenny, for introducing me to the horror genre far sooner than could ever be deemed responsible for a child my age.

# ACKNOWLEDGMENTS

I would like to thank my wife, Sian, for her support and
patience in gifting me the time to write my stories.
I would like to thank my two little creatures of the night,
Sophia and Carys, for finding ways to simultaneously keep
me sane and drive me mad.
I would like to thank my family for their constant support
and encouragement.
I would like to thank my brothers from other mothers,
Rob, Karl, Kev, Dan, and Lloyd for allowing me to
bounce ideas off them and for their feedback and honesty.
Finally, I would like to thank anyone who has ever picked
up, read, or listened to one of my books. Without your
support, this book would not exist.

# OCTOBER 28, 1985

# 1

The flash of light and clap of thunder was strong enough to awaken the teenage boy from his deep slumber.

Any questions his muddled mind may have had about the hour of the night were soon answered by another flare of sheet lightning. The flash may have only lasted for a minuscule moment, yet it had still been sufficient to illuminate the room. Enough for Willard Jennings to observe the clock that hung on the wall opposing his single bed. The time was five minutes past three in the morning.

The inevitable roll of thunder then came.

The lull between this booming crash and its predecessor didn't seem long at all. The eye of the storm must surely have been close overhead of Bleddington - the small, southern English town in which he had lived throughout his fourteen years of life.

The barrage of heavy rain was relentless in its onslaught against the besieged pane of the bedroom window, causing him to question how he had managed to sleep through the intrusive noise in the first place.

The burning curiosity, which was a mandatory character trait for his age, urged him to get up and observe this almighty storm. Yet, the intrigue was soon quelled into submission by the dominant part of him that was simply too tired to get out of bed at this heinous hour.

Another flash came. This time, however, Willard's eyes weren't focused on the clock.

He was sure he had caught a glimpse of something, no, someone, standing at the foot of the bedroom wall.

Though he was expecting it, the clap of thunder still caused him to jolt. The storm was even louder now, more so than any he could ever remember hearing before.

He dismissed the image he'd thought he'd seen as the calamitous cocktail of tired eyes, coupled with a groggy mind.

Then the next illumination came. This was not tired eyes. This was not his imagination.

The figure was facing him. Only, this time, it was one step closer towards his bed. Though the lightning flash was brief, he had still seen enough to torment his mind.

The next thunderclap barely registered, despite being, somehow, even louder.

The figure he'd seen was of a child's height. It wore a girl's, red, knee-high winter coat, and yellow wellington boots. Yet, it was her face that stood out the most - or, chillingly, the lack of one.

A white porcelain mask dominated the dark space between the coat's hood. A large crack trailed down the left-hand side of the china veil.

The next cameo of light came much quicker now.

The figure was at the foot of the bed.

Willard felt paralysed through fear. Not even a scream could escape his open mouth, nor could he even wipe the tears forming in his eyes.

The phantasm had been near enough for him to gaze briefly into the black void where its eyes should have been behind the mask

A steady flow of urine seeped through the boy's pyjama bottoms and through to the duvet.

He closed his eyes tightly, hoping this would be enough to deter this spectre from coming any closer.

It wasn't.

He wished that the cracking sound was the rain, striking hard against the sheet of glass, yet the noise was coming from within the room. It was coming from above his bed.

The Girl with a Porcelain Face

Willard could feel the figure crawling over him. The sound of snapping bones played in unison with each chilling movement as it crept atop the soaked duvet. The scratching sensation sickened him as he could feel a jagged object scraping along his torso.

The intruder inched closer to his face.

He determined from the position of the sharp tip grazing against him that this wasn't a blade, but splintered bone protruding from the figure's broken body.

Despite every instinct pleading with him not to, he forced his stinging, tear-filled eyes to open.

The lightning struck one last time.

Her face was atop his. The sound of sobbing coming from behind the porcelain mask was loud enough to rival that of the boy.

Whereas Willard's whimpers were of terror, the apparitions were of pain.

Then, the silence came.

The storm had ended.

She was gone.

# 2

Whenever Patricia Weyland was asked by the Bleddington townsfolk to name the things she didn't like about her job as the cleaner to Hilltop Manor, her instant response would always be, "the arduous walk up the steep flight of concrete steps embedded into the hill." Upon the summit of which, the large, ten-bedroom Victorian manor stood, dominating the view above the small tin-mining town.

She was also just as quick to clarify, much to the displeasure of her variety of nosey interrogators, that this was just about the only thing she didn't like about her employment.

Her employer, Royston Jennings, had always been nothing but good to her. He paid far more than he should have, out of choice, and had always treated her as one of the family. Not that he had much in the way of family to speak of, aside from his son Willard - whom she adored.

In her twenty years of service to Hilltop Manor, she'd grown to become rather protective of them both, despite the hatred many of the townsfolk held for the elder Jennings.

Mrs Weyland had never been more grateful for the handrail that had been fixed alongside the steps to cling onto, as it was proving to be slippery underfoot following the heinous storm of the night before. It was an additional hurdle her sixty-three-year-old body could do without on this cold Autumn morning.

She twisted her front door key into the keyhole and proceeded to hang her thick winter jacket upon the antique brass coat stand located at the mouth of the large hall dominated by the site of a black, cast iron, spiral staircase that led to the upper level of the home. She then made her way to the east wing of the manor, and to the dining room,

where, most often, Royston would be found at this
hour.

True to expectation, her employer was sitting at the
dining table, head deep in the daily newspaper.

As much as she found her thrice-weekly ascent up the
hill arduous, she felt more pity for the town's paperboy.
That poor sucker had to make this expedition every
morning, and at an ungodly hour to boot. At least he had
the consolation of being able to boast calf muscles even a
mountain goat would be envious of by the time he'd
achieved his early retirement from the paper-delivering
profession.

Willard was sitting opposite his father, headphones on,
listening to his Bush Walkman. Neither of them was
acknowledging the other's presence, yet this was more out
of a long-played-out habit than any spiteful intentions.

Mrs Weyland had often observed that their relationship
was a strange and distant one.

"Good morning, my handsome men," she greeted
chipperly, trying to inject some much-needed enthusiasm
into the room.

"Morning, Mrs Weyland," Royston's languid return
came. He didn't even look up from the newspaper, sapping
away any of the energy gifted to him in the process. Not
that she held it against him. She never did.

Before the sudden closure of the tin mine, Royston had
been a driven man. For better, and very often, for worse,
he had been filled with a fight to succeed. Mrs Weyland
suspected it had been to prove wrong those who merely
saw him as someone fortunate enough to inherit the
business, and its substantial fortunes, at such a premature
age - rather than it being taken over by a person more
qualified and worthy.

It was his drive to succeed that made it surprising to her, and everyone else in the town, when it was Royston himself who decided to close down the mine a couple of years ago, with abruptness and without an explanation.

Even had he chosen to sell it, that would have made business sense, such was the mine's worth. But to shut it down completely and halt all operations within a month, defied all rationale.

Even though most of his riches remained, Royston had seemingly lost the will to prove everyone wrong about himself. If anything, he had validated their disfavour of him. Only now, he wasn't just disapproved of by the townsfolk of Bleddington - he was despised.

Willard, at least, was more forthcoming in his greeting to the cleaner and displayed some etiquette beyond his teenage years by removing his headphones.

Patricia couldn't help but have already noticed the boy's bloodshot eyes, underscored by the puffy bags of skin underneath. She could tell he'd had little to no sleep, yet she chose not to press him on the matter.

Having two children herself that had navigated the tumultuous epoch of adolescence, she knew from experience that, just the slightest pressing of personal matters, would feel like a Spanish Inquisition in comparison.

"What are you listening to?" she instead asked with disguised interest, despite holding no doubt that whatever the answer would be, she wouldn't have heard of them.

"Just some Foreigner," he replied groggily.

"Oh, you mean like Julio Iglesias or something?" her innocent but misguided reply came.

Willard knew he could correct her and explain who the band was, but he didn't have either the energy, patience, nor the enthusiasm on this morning.

Trying to describe the current music scene to the cleaner would be as futile as someone attempting to describe different colours to somebody born blind. Besides, the music may have been blasting into his ears, rapidly draining his set of Eveready batteries in the process, but he wasn't paying any attention to it.

Willard still couldn't get his vivid nightmare from the early hours of the morning out of his mind; and by this juncture, that's all he had convinced himself it was. After all, logic, sanity, and hope, dictated that it couldn't possibly be anything else.

"Mrs Weyland, could I ask you something please?" he muttered discretely enough not to draw the attention of his father. Not that he doubted it would have made much of a difference, since he was so entrenched in his copy of the Daily Telegraph.

"Of course, Will," Patricia boomed with an enthusiasm and excess volume that instantly negated the clandestine nature of Willard's request.

The boy let out a purposeful heavy-handed sigh to show his frustration, then gestured for the cleaner to follow him to the grand hall.

"Are you okay, Will?" she asked with genuine concern.

"Yes, I'm fine. Just, well, a little embarrassed really. It's about my bedroom."

A reassuring smile began to find its way onto Mrs Weyland's weathered and worried face. She thought she knew where this conversation was heading.

"If it's about those dirty magazines I found under your bed, then there's no need to worry. I won't mention them to your father. If I may say though, you have come a long way since the Beano."

"No, it's not about those Mrs Weyland. It's just that, well, I had a little accident in my bed last night and I need my bedding cleaned and dried without my father finding out."

"The storm shook you up a bit, did it?"

"Something like that."

"Rest assured; I'll take care of it."

Willard smiled his gratitude to the cleaner before grabbing his school bag from the foot of the coat stand.

"Hey," he called out in an effort to draw his father's eyes away from the page. "I'm off to school now."

"Okay," Royston responded with little interest. Willard often found his father's indifference to him infuriating, but today, with his emotions frayed from the lack of sleep, it only served to amplify his vexation.

"Yeah, I'll probably end up robbing a shop on the way, maybe knock some girl up, then I'm thinking of getting a tattoo of a swastika on my right arm."

"Don't get smart, son." His father countered in the same droll manner, adding to his son's aggravation.

If there was any consolation for Willard at this rebuttal, at least it meant his father was listening to his words. Perhaps he wasn't the oblivious zombie he took him for.

# 3

Ten minutes or so passed since Willard left the house, and Mrs Weyland was upstairs, making a start on the numerous upper-level rooms. Such was the size of the house, it wasn't so much a task for the first floor to be cleaned before lunchtime, but a heroic quest.

Royston's heart skipped a vital beat as the tranquillity of the moment became broken by a sudden and loud ringing of the telephone.

He coaxed his nearly-fifty-year-old body up from the chair, carefully placing the newspaper open upon the table so as not to lose his page. Part of him hoped the phone would stop with the same abruptness as it had started so he wouldn't be forced to converse with anyone. Yet, it continued to ring belligerently.

"Royston Jennings speaking," he greeted robotically.

He recognised the voice on the other end of the line as soon as he spoke. It belonged to Solomon Fisher, his best friend since childhood. These days that title became bestowed upon him purely by default. Royston didn't have many other friends to speak of, nor to.

"Hi, old pal," the familiar, but cautious speech came.

Jennings sensed something was afoot. Not just because Solomon seldom spoke to him anymore, but due to his hesitant tone. Despite Solomon's occupation as the town Undertaker, his demeanour was usually about as puckish as they came.

"Sol, is everything okay?"

"She's back!"

The call ended.

10

# 4

Dominic Drakeford and Thomas Greene had been waiting, as they almost always did, at the head of the public footpath adjoining the base of the hill, ready to greet their friend upon his descent from his impressive home.

Willard had always thought it counter-productive for his two best friends - his only friends - to convene with him at this spot, since it meant them doubling back and adding another ten minutes, or so, onto their commute to school as a consequence.

When they had first struck up their friendship, Drake and Tommy were extremely eager to meet him at this spot at the behest of curiosity, as it resulted in getting a closer view of the magnificent manor on top of it.

After a while, however, it had become as much their unwavering routine, as it was for Willard to point out the flaws of their adopted meeting place.

On this morning though, traditions would be broken.

Drake and Tommy conveyed their greetings, as per usual, anticipating Willard to tell them, in parrot fashion, 'You know you don't have to wait for me here. We literally walk past your houses on our route, I can call for you. It would be so much easier.'

This exact conversation wasn't just a ritual now, but a running joke.

Today, however, their salutations were met with a prolonged and ignorant silence, followed by the anti-climax that was a distant grunt of acknowledgement.

"Someone's gotten out of the wrong side of bed this morning," Drake mocked, hoping to bring some form of equilibrium to their routine.

"Nah, he's just confused because he's finally started puberty," Tommy was quick to interject, to which he was greeted by a high-five from Drake, and yet more silence from Willard.

Insults and mockery were a regular trait among the trio of friends. The only thing off limits between them was mum jokes, due to Drake and Willard both losing theirs. Willard had never met his owing to a fatal heart attack during childbirth, and Dominic's was at only five years old, caused by blunt force trauma from a heavy fall.

Resided by the fact they had lost Willard's contribution to the daily banter, Drake and Tommy partook amongst themselves in the obligatory talking of complete and utter bollocks, which at their youthful age they mistook for being deeply profound.

"Did you see Children's BBC yesterday evening, Tommy?"

"No. I'm fourteen, I have a life now. I was busy all night playing Ghostbusters on my C64. I made it past the Marshmallow Man on the end level."

"Bullshit, no one makes it past the Marshmallow Man."

"I'm telling you I did. I swear on my mother's li....... I promise."

"Well, had you been watching Children's BBC yesterday afternoon you would have seen some tits," Drake spoke with misguided pride.

"Now whose calling bullshit?"

"I swear. It was a new cartoon called Thundercats. Some sexy cat-type woman by the name of Cheetara was naked I tell you. Granted, she had no nipples. But, for a while, she was proper in the nude."

"You need to find yourself a girlfriend buddy," Tommy's dry but sincere response came. "Oh, look, there's a stray cat across the road, do you want to shag that too?"

The conversation for the next few minutes seldom elevated from this juvenile level, yet this was to change as they approached Court Street, opposite the school entrance.

Even had Willard not been so predisposed in thought, it would have been unlikely he'd have seen the incoming football, propelling towards him at speed, in time to avoid it as it collided with full force against the side of his face.

The three friends scanned over in symmetry towards the direction which the inflated projectile had come from. They were not surprised to see a group of older kids, aged fifteen, standing behind Nathanial Finch. They doubted now that the ball to the face had been an innocuous accident.

Finch was the worst of combinations at that age. Not only was he the school bully, able to back himself in any fight, but he was also a spoilt, rich, brat full of self-entitlement.

Nathanial's father, Huxley Finch, was an entrepreneur, and owner of several stores and businesses throughout Bleddington. It had been heavily rumoured he had his sticky hands in numerous other enterprises too, but never anything official enough for the taxman to tie him down to.

It had always been a mystery to Willard, and many others too he presumed, as to why Nathanial was slumming it in Bleddington Comprehensive School when he should have been gaining his education in a fancy boarding school in some location more desirable.

Whenever he thought on this perplexity, however, he tried not to dwell on it too hard since the same situation applied to himself. He'd never even ventured outside of the town for more than a few hours at a time. His father wasn't keeping him around for regular and in-depth conversations, that was for sure.

From Willard's understanding, his father and Huxley Finch had been close friends in their younger years, yet this affiliation had never been shared by their sons.

"Nice header, Jennings," Finch mocked to a round of sniggers from his entourage. "Pass the ball back fuckface."

Drake didn't say anything as he claimed the ball from Willard. He didn't need to. Tommy and Willard recognised all too well the expression on his face.

Despite the banter and insults he was eager to dish out with aplomb to his friends, he was also fiercely protective should anyone else try to mess with them. On many occasions he'd had to fend off Willard's numerous schoolyard adversaries for him, often with mixed success.

The smirk upon Drake's face suggested he was about to do something regrettable.

"Whatever you've got in mind, don't. It's not worth it," Willard attempted to reason. It may have been his first meaningful contribution to the conversation so far this morning. Yet, in this instance, it was a case of quality over quantity.

Drake's mischievous smile expanded further in response to these wise words. He glanced down and observed some dog mess on the patch of grass in front of them. He had been gifted too much of a perfect opportunity to squander.

For right or wrong, the guiding stars of tomfoolery had aligned for him. Sure, the aftermath would be hazardous to his health, but the immediate gratification would be worth it. It was the equivalent of a type-1 diabetic winning a golden ticket to Willy Wonka's chocolate factory.

Drake placed the football on the grass adjoining the pavement and, with his foot, he discretely rolled the ball over the dog turd. The storm of the night before ensured the animal excrement remained unpleasantly wet and sticky.

Drake composed himself to punt the ball back. Such was his concentration and focus, he couldn't hear his friend's protests now, even if he wanted to.

"You want it, you got it," he shouted to the hoods.

The kick was a precise one. He had executed it with perfection. Drake could picture their P.E teacher, Mr Hudson, berating him with a frustrated pride, "why can't you do that on a football field, Drakeford?"

Though the contaminated ball was kicked at speed, the three friends viewed it hurtling towards the bully as if in a slow-motion replay from Match of the Day. Right up to the point where Finch performed an instinctive header to control the object.

It wasn't so much egg on the bully's face, but something far-less savoury.

The stunned silence soon turned into a chorus of disgusted repugnance, followed by a Mexican-Wave of giggles as an increasing number of the commuting children passing by the scene of the incident began to realise what had happened.

The only ones not to see the funny side were Finch, Tommy, and Willard. They knew only too well what was about to happen.

Finch would have to dish out an almighty reckoning, and Tommy and Willard would suffer the ordeal of watching their friend on the receiving end.

"Run!" Tommy ordered. Yet the bully already had the advantage of a running start and superior speed.

Drake retreated to the closest thing constituting as diplomatic immunity as he made it through the school gates.

The sanctuary of the schoolyard didn't stop Finch from pouncing upon him, however. He rugby-tackled his prey to the floor and used the tie of his victim's school uniform to wipe the smeared patch of dog shit from his forehead before stuffing the soiled end into Drake's mouth.

"Think you're bloody funny do you, Drakeford? Let's see how funny you find things when you're drinking your meals through a straw after I knock your teeth out."

"What's going on here?" An adult voice spoke with an assertive calm as he brushed his way through the amassing gathering of pupils waiting to witness the beating. "Finch! Why am I not surprised? Get off him. Now."

Both Finch and Drake panned up and laid eyes upon the tall and slender figure of the English teacher, Mr Kready, standing above them.

"He started it," Finch exclaimed.

"And I'm finishing it," Kready affirmed. "Now, are you going to make me repeat myself? Get - off - him."

The middle-aged teacher may have appeared gaunt and perpetually ill with his pale face, thinning hair, and sunken eyes, yet something about him intimidated Finch. He almost never raised his voice in temper, no matter how much some of the other pupils tried to push him, but something about the disdain in which he stared at Finch suggested he incontrovertibly loathed him.

"Yes sir," Finch submitted as he relinquished his grip on Drake's collar and stood to his feet. "This ain't over," he whispered as he did so.

"Are you okay, Dominic?" the teacher inquired in a tone which perceived he held the child in more favourable regard.

"Yes sir," Drake eventually confirmed after coughing out the tie and retching upon the contrasting fresh air. Tommy and Willard joined their friend to help him up.

"A word of advice Dominic," Kready continued. "When you pour gasoline onto a fire, it will almost always blow up in your face."

The teacher's gaze turned over to Willard, the cold stare he gave him indicated he was another of the pupils he had a loathing for, and he never attempted to hide this fact.

Kready's glance lingered on him for longer than was necessary before concluding with a sympathetic glance back at Drake.

"Get yourself cleaned up, then get to registration. I don't want to see you three again until your morning classes."

# 5

Royston knocked upon the front door of the Bleddington Funeral Parlour.

It was a building he had been inside many times growing up due to his childhood friendship with the undertaker's son, Solomon Fisher.

When he had been a youngster, he'd thought of it as a place of great intrigue. Yet, once the naivety of adolescence had abandoned him, and he had been sucker-punched by that asshole called adulthood, coming here on more occasions than he cared for, brought with it a great deal of distress. None more so than when he'd come to visit the resting place of his late wife, Constance.

Hearing the unexpected phone call from his friend this morning, however, brought with it duress of a different kind.

No response came to the initial round of polite knocking. A part of Royston implored himself to just turn around and retreat to the comparative comforts of Hilltop Manor.

The residual piece of fight remaining inside of him, which hated conceding defeat, forced him to stay, however. He continued with his knocking until he had his answer. His next round of rapping at the door displayed far more purpose.

"Alright, I'm coming." A flustered voice came from within the parlour. "If you carry on making a commotion like that, you'll wake the dead, and that is not a good business practice when you are an undertaker."

The door opened.

Standing in the ingress was a portly, balding, middle-aged man. He wore a Hawaiian shirt, tie-dyed red jeans, and sported a 70s porn star moustache. He was as far removed from the archetypal image of a mortician as one would expect.

Since he was the town's sole funeral director, however, he offered the townsfolk little choice but to go to him for their inevitable business - and he was damned if he was going to change for anyone. Besides, no one ever dared with sincerity deny that when it came to the funeral services themselves, he was as professional, meticulous, and as appropriately dressed as one could ask for.

Royston couldn't help but observe in Solomon's right hand was an open bottle of Jamesons Whiskey. It looked to be close to empty.

"I had an inkling I'd lay eyes upon you this morning, my old chum," the undertaker greeted with no shortage of gusto.

"A little bit early to be drinking, isn't it?" Royston lectured in response.

"On the contrary, my dear man, I am, as a matter of fact, way behind schedule. I intended on starting last night but I was somewhat preoccupied."

"You said in your call, she was back." Royston cut straight to the chase. As much as he wanted to catch up in the proper manner with his friend and talk about happier times from what seemed a time long ago now, the words he had spoken on the abrupt phone call held far more precedence.

Solomon ushered his visitor inside with haste, he didn't want to run the risk of their conversation being listened upon. Not by anyone alive at least.

"Be careful what you say, Roy," Solomon spoke with an evident nervousness. He had now abandoned the bluster of his previous demeanour. "You know the consequences of saying her name."

Royston took the bottle from the undertaker and took a heavy swig for himself. He knew the consequences more than anyone.

"Did you see...her? Taking extra care not to say the name aloud."

"Not exactly, but I have someone out back who did. You're welcome to question them as much as you like though, my dear. But I must warn you, he's been quite the silent type as of late."

Royston threw Sol a look to suggest his morbid sense of undertaker humour wasn't being appreciated right now.

Solomon led him out to the cool room where his 'clients' were awaiting their funeral service, causing a flood of memories to come surging back.

Looking back at it now, his childhood gang's shenanigans, practical jokes, and outright dumb fuckery – of which there'd been plentiful - was nothing but juvenile and disrespectful. Plus, their hijinks often resulted in them getting their hides tanned. On occasion, however, some of the results had been worth the ten licks with the belt.

Despite the gravitas of the situation, Royston let out an inadvertent giggle as he remembered the time Sol and himself had pranked their good friend, Huxley Finch.

Upon visiting Sol for an afterschool hangout, little was he aware, Royston was already in the parlour - and hidden inside an empty casket.

As he listened to his friends' footsteps entering the chamber, he took that as his queue to begin messing with Hux.

"Hello, is someone there?" he called out in a disguised, staged and petrified, voice. "Where...where am I? The last thing I remember was having severe pains in my chest. Then, it was darkness."

Royston battled hard with himself not to break character and burst out laughing, as he could hear through the coffin, Huxley's frightened gasps.

Sol, who was the composer of this prank was conducting Hux with aplomb with his staged astonishment.

"No way, man. This can't be happening," Sol freaked.

Looking back at it now, his acting would best be described as enthusiastic, but at the time, both he and Royston were convinced they'd enacted Oscar-worthy performances.

"Your dad's gone and put a live person in the coffin by accident!" Huxley spoke with distressed concern.

"Impossible," Sol countered, maintaining his charade. "They're certified deceased by the doctor's way before they come here. If it's in a coffin it's dead, you can mark my words."

"It's so cold," Royston projected after allowing a prolonged moment for Sol's words to digest with Hux. "It's so dark, and so cold. I can't feel a thing."

"Jesus, Mary, Joseph, and that little fucking donkey they rode in on," Huxley whimpered. "Let's get the hell out of here."

"I'm hungry," the voice from the coffin came. "So hungry. I - crave - blood."

"Holy shit!" one of the voices squealed from outside the coffin.

The bait had been taken. Now was his time to further reel him in.

Royston started groaning as he slowly lifted the coffin lid.

The look on his friend's face during that taunting moment between fear and realisation was one Sol and he would remind him of every chance they had for a long time. The triumph of the prank was almost enough to help distract Sol from the pain of the lashing he took once word of his antics had gotten back to his father.

The smile of recollection soon turned to a mien of moroseness as his thoughts turned to Sol's father, Franklyn Fisher. He was a cantankerous, intimidating, and short-tempered man. The sympathetic side of Royston tried to convince himself that Franklyn didn't deserve to die the way he did. The more realistic side of him knew this wasn't the case though. For what they had done that night, they all deserved it.

Solomon must have second-guessed some of the emotions taking up residence inside his visitor's mind, but he didn't seek to acknowledge them. One of the things undertakers are good at is burying things - memories included.

He ushered his friend to a casket and opened it. Royston recognized the corpse inside in an instant. His name was Daniel Harker.

Daniel, the son of the Bleddington police sergeant, had been in their year at school and hung out with them on occasion, though he would never be classed as one of their gang.

"He was found at the bottom of his stairs with a broken neck and spine. The poor bastard had already been dead for a few days. He had no surviving family, and no real friends anymore. It was only when the odours were starting to seep through to outside the house, and into the garden, his neighbour put in a call of concern to the police. They found some open bottles of spirits in his bedroom and say the drink must have caused the fall."

"You think it's her though, don't you? You said it yourself, she's back. Did he mention anything to you before the...accident?"

"I haven't spoken to Harker for months," Sol sought to clarify. "Even then, it was only a polite acknowledgement when we passed each other around town. We were almost strangers these days. As far as I know, he didn't leave any notes or messages for us to find, but there was no need for one. A dead person's face tells a tale more detailed than any letter ever could.

Words lie, my dear, but the deceased's resting face is as honest a missive as you will ever see in this world. You've just got to learn how to read them, and when you've been around my business for as long as I have, rest assured, I am very well-read.

It wasn't drinking that caused his fall, it was fear."

Royston wasn't sure how to react to his friend's statement, he wasn't even sure how much of it he believed.

Was this just some unfocused paranoia, coupled with an unhealthy amount of drink at such an unruly hour? Was it years of suppressed guilt of what happened thirty years ago seeping through to the surface?

Either way, Sol was playing a dangerous game. Even making mention of... her, risked bringing dangerous repercussions to themselves.

# 6

Monday morning at 09:30 meant one thing for the pupils of Bleddington Comprehensive, regardless of what class or year they were in. This was the timeslot reserved for the weekly school assembly.

The students robotically filed into the school hall and, with little enthusiasm, sat themselves on the wooden floor.

Without fail, what would always start as a gentle ripple of conversation between a splattering of children would soon turn into a tsunami of chatter before the headmaster, Mr Grenfield, was due to take the stage.

One of the many pockets of dialogue struggling to be heard amongst the chaotic choir of voices belonged to Willard, Drake, and Tommy.

"So, Will," Tommy pressed with his customary bluntness. "Are you going to tell us what's been going on with you this morning? If you were any more distant, you'd need to have a passport to come back to us."

"Sorry guys," Willard responded with sincerity. "It's, well, I had a hell of a nightmare last night and it shook me up bad. Not even Rowdy Roddy Piper could be able to wrestle it out of my mind. It was so vivid."

"Why didn't you tell us this earlier?" Tommy probed further. "It would have been far more interesting than having to listen to Drake bang on about a cartoon cat with tits."

"I don't know, honestly. It sounds just as strange now I'm saying it aloud as it is that I'm thinking it, but I have this feeling in the pit of my stomach that I shouldn't be talking about, the girl with a porcelain face, from my nightmare. Crazy, right?"

Drake and Tommy's concern switched to intrigue upon hearing this statement. The captivated expressions became etched on their faces, as they stared absorbedly at their friend, making it impossible for him to refuse further elaboration.

Before he had the chance to commence his recounting of what had been troubling him with so much malevolence, a new voice could be heard throughout the assembly room. It belonged to Mr Grenfield.

"Silence," the booming voice commanded. Instant silence he received. "Let us begin this morning's assembly with the Lord's Prayer."

The gathering began to regurgitate the prayer with a droning monotony. Some recitals of the passage were more accurate than others, due to several of the pupils taking inevitable liberties with their interpretation.

'Our Father who Fart's in Heaven,' was an obvious variation. Another was adding far more emphasis on the **ass** in tresp**ass**.

The prayer ended, and the headmaster seamlessly transitioned into a meandering monologue. It was an unsubtle attempt to shoehorn his love of religious parables into the guise of a current event.

His speech was cut short, however, by the sight of the school secretary, Miss Hamley, awkwardly entering the room and making a beeline to the front of the stage. She beckoned him towards her, so she could speak quietly in his ear.

"Pardon me, children," he boomed, before adding the caveat, "this is not an excuse for you to start talking amongst yourselves."

The secretary's shaken demeanour was transmitted in an instant onto his. Whatever news being delivered to the headmaster, was clearly not of a favourable kind. His face had turned ashen before its conclusion.

Mr Grenfield was visibly distressed as he anxiously surveyed the room, trying to pick out one of the pupils. His gaze came to a sudden halt.

"Nathanial Finch," His voice struggled. "Can you go with Miss Hamley to the main office please?"

Willard had never seen the school bully so vulnerable before. All eyes in the room instinctively fell upon him. His confident swagger had eroded into a nervous walk as he left the room under the secretary's escort.

"Do you think Kready said something about your skirmish?" Tommy asked Drake.

"Maybe," he answered with a thinly veiled solemnness. "But this has got nothing to do with that."

To say there was no love lost between Finch and himself would be an understatement, yet he felt a bond of understanding for his adversary during this moment.

"I've seen that look before," Drake elaborated. "It was the same as my old headmaster gave me when I was five years old. When he found out my mother had died."

# 7

Royston was ambling along his favoured route through the streets of Bleddington, which would, in due course, join onto the footpath leading to the base of Hilltop Manor.

It wasn't the shortest way home, nor was it the most picturesque, yet it brought with it a sense of nostalgia from his childhood days. A time, for him, when life appeared simpler.

Despite the memories of times far happier trying to worm their way to the forefront of his mind, they were smothered with little resistance by the troubling thoughts weighing heavy upon him.

Then he saw it.

As he exited Brook Avenue, he could view from the corner of his peripheral, a glimpse of the main road.

It wasn't so much the sight of the road which had caught his attention, but the huddle of people chatting animatedly amongst themselves at the side of the curb.

The flash of yellow police tape encircled what looked to be a Ford Sierra. Even from this distance, his eyes could make out what looked to be heavy windscreen damage, infused with a splattering of blood and other clotted matter.

Despite having no desire to interact with the inhabitants of the town, no more so since the likelihood was he'd either put them or their family out of work, he still found himself drawn to the scene of the accident. He felt as compelled as a moth drawn to a bright light.

"What happened?" he asked, despite the obviousness of the answer. What he really meant to say was, "whom has this happened to?"

The chatter amongst the huddle turned to a gradual and awkward silence upon the residents realising Royston's presence. A few of them even left the scene of the accident, to further demonstrate their dislike of this man - just in case of any such doubt.

Of those who remained, a middle-aged lady by the name of Hazel Yardly, was only too glad to give her description.

She had seen the incident first-hand, half an hour earlier, and had stayed ever since, revelling in the limelight of being able to give her account to anyone who passed, whether they wanted it or not.

"I've never seen anything like it," she declared for dramatic effect.

She'd had so much practice in recounting the accident by this point, she'd had her narrative delivery down to a fine art.

"It was Huxley Finch. He was walking down the street, lording over the place as he so often did. When, all of a sudden, he started freaking out over something. I mean, one minute he was his usual smug self, the next he was panicking, apologising, and screaming for forgiveness. He was shouting to someone, yet nobody was there. I swear on my life. The next thing I saw was him backing away as if something was coming towards him. Unfortunately, for Mister Finch, may God bless his soul, he backed away into the road and straight into that Sierra. It wasn't the poor driver's fault. No way could he have braked in time."

Hazel couldn't help but detect the shaken look drawn on Royston's face.

"Oh, Mr Jennings. I am so sorry. He was a friend of yours, wasn't he?"

"Huh?" came the distant response.

"I said you two were friends, weren't you?"

"Oh, er, yes," he confirmed distantly. "A long time ago, at least."

"You have my condolences," she continued. Not that Royston heard what she had said. He had continued with his walk, and now he was even deeper in troubling thoughts.

Sol was right, she was back.

"I've never seen anything like it," Hazel began again as the next person came into her eye-line.

# 8

Mr Kready's English classes were often a sterile experience.

The format of his lessons followed the same tedious, unfulfilling path with fervent frequency. He would hand out a copy of whatever book took his fancy that day, and one seldom on the curriculum, before electing a pupil to read out a chapter from it before handing over to the classmate at the adjacent desk, to narrate the next. It was the literary equivalent of Russian Roulette as to whether you would be forced to read or not.

Sometimes, the novels he'd choose would have chapters long enough to ensure only one or two pupils would be called upon to read in that lesson. Other times, the books would have short enough passages to call upon a dozen or so to partake.

If you were one of the fortunate, who didn't have to recite the pages, the lessons were a daydreamer's paradise. If you were one of the unlucky, you could lay claim to being a victim of futility, since no one, let alone Mr Kready, paid any meaningful attention to the recital.

To taunt them further, on occasion when he'd brought in a book which was unanimous in its enjoyment, they'd never finish it, since the next lesson he would be guaranteed to bring in another. The pupils would have to seek out the book themselves from the library, or order it from the town's small bookshop, if they wanted to read it to the end. Some speculated this had been his cunning ploy all along.

Sometimes, however, Kready would surprise them all and actually teach, or, at the very least, engage with them. The tragedy was, that on the occasions when the mood took him, he was a perfectly proficient teacher. Today was one of those days.

"I have an assignment for you all to complete for when you return from Autumn half term," he spoke, catching the class off guard. "I want you to choose an event from this town's history and write a short story about it. Remember, this is an English class, not History. The prose doesn't have to be accurate. If mass embellishment is good enough for Hollywood, it's good enough for this classroom. All I ask is that your piece is well-written, not riddled with grammatical errors, and appropriate for you to read out loud to the rest of your peers.

If you're stuck for anything of interest that's happened in this town and, quite frankly, I can't say I blame you, fear not. I have procured some old editions of the Bleddington Gazette from an old friend. You may be interested to know that, back in the day, when I wouldn't have been much older than you lot are now, I even helped out using the printing press during my school holidays. Though, I can tell by the lack of enthralment on your delightful faces, that none of you have appeared interested to know that at all.

In any case, you are free to borrow a copy. Now, when I say borrow, that is precisely what I mean. I want them brought back in the exact condition you've taken them in. This means no using the pages for origami experiments, no using the paper as bedding for your beloved-but-pointless pet hamster, and no drawing Hitler moustaches or reproductive organs over the photographs. I'll be taking a register of who has which edition, so any shenanigans will be easily traceable. Got it?"

"Yes, sir!" the class recited unenthusiastically in unison, as much out of habit, as from having any opportunity for hijinks with the newspapers being thwarted at the first hurdle.

"Come and collect your papers from the pile in desk order."

Such was the shroud of intimidation Kready held over his class, there was little talking amongst them as they queued up to receive their newspaper from the uniformly arranged stacks upon his desk.

Many of the class often joked in the playground, and out of earshot of the English teacher, that even the bogeyman checked underneath his bed for Mr Kready before he went to sleep.

Willard's turn came to collect his newspaper from the desk. No words were spoken between the teacher and himself, just a festering silence.

Willard had never been sure as to why Mr Kready resented him. He was a model pupil, a joy to teach, as many of the other teachers would remark in their school reports. Yet Kready's intense gaze would always feel like it was burning a hole through his soul.

"Next," he declared.

Willard took this as his cue to return to his desk and allow Tommy, who was standing behind him, to pick up his gazette.

Once returning to their desks, Willard observed the front of his copy. The date upon it was October 18th, 1937. He had hit the jackpot.

The page displayed the news of a near-fatal accident in the tin mine. He already had a strong enough starting point to inspire a story.

Willard was disrupted from thoughts of his assignment by Tommy's voice whispering from the desk next to him.

"Hey, Will! Wanna trade?"

Willard glanced over to the adjacent desk and peered over at Tommy's paper, which he was suspiciously obscuring with his forearm. He opted for an interrogating glance as he locked eyes with his friend. It was effective enough a look to make Tommy sigh and move his arm to reveal what he had purposely been hiding.

Willard scoffed aloud as if to say, 'nice try sunshine.'

On his front page was the less-than-dramatic headline of 'stepladder stolen from vicar's garden.' It must have been a slow Newsday that week, even by Bleddington's dreary standards.

Willard lifted his paper off the desk and angled it so his friend could see the superior headline. He even mimicked laughing at him in a mocking manner, like a maniacal Bond villain, before flipping him the finger for extra measure.

Despite having the perfect starting point for a story, out of curiosity, he still proceeded to read the rest of the paper.

He only made it to page 3 and the image that dominated it.

This picture may not have been as glamorous or as easy to look at as those he and his friends always snuck a peak at on page 3 of the Sun at their local newsagents. It may not have been Linda Lusardi, Sam Fox, or Mariah Whitaker, yet the subject of the photo was one he recognised in an instant. It was his grandfather, Wilbur Jennings.

Willard knew little about his grandfather, other than he had died from a successful suicide long before Willard was born. Successful suicide! He had found this term to be an odd choice of words. Shouldn't a failed attempt be seen as more of a success in the long run?

Whenever Willard had asked his father about his grandfather, he was liable to change the subject or, more often, shut him down completely.

Nonetheless, traces of him were still scattered around Hilltop Manor. Most notable was a masterfully painted portrait of him still hanging in the study.

The photograph Willard was staring at with amazement was of his grandfather standing in front of Hilltop Manor. He was a handsome, middle-aged man. The proud and beaming smile he displayed made Willard wonder how someone with such joy on his face and success in his life could have been desperate enough to have ended it. Above the photo, the headline read.

Wilbur Jennings to open the doors of Hilltop Manor to his employees for Halloween Party.

The article wrote of how, as a thank you to his miners and their families for the prosperity the mine was bringing him, he was hosting what he intended to be an annual Halloween party in his grand home.

Like most small-town news that had been relegated to the inner pages of its earnest local paper, this was hardly an earth-shattering story. Yet, to Willard, this throwaway story excited him far more than the dramatic near-fatal mining accident.

To think his home, which almost never received any visitors, seldom heard any laughter, and certainly never entertained any excitement during his time of living there, was host to what he imagined to be grandioso parties, filled with guests and revelry.

Willard needed to know more and was sure his father would have at least some knowledge of them. He would ask him this evening.

# 9

The time was coming up to 11:00 and Royston had just returned to his home upon the hill.

The thoughts of heading back to the funeral parlour instead, to inform Sol first-hand of their friend's passing - and the troubling witness account of how it happened - submerged his mind. Yet, he fought against it.

Sol would discover soon enough about the accident. Even had death not been his profession, the speed in which news travelled in this town meant word of Huxley's passing was more liable to reach him even before Royston did. Besides, Sol knew how and where to find him.

He made his way across the manor's hall, to the west wing and the small library located at the end of the corridor. He carried with him the intention of immersing himself in some reading of the antique books contained within the impressive room. He hoped the pages of whatever prose he would choose would transport his distracted mind far away, and he didn't care what places his imagination took him. Anywhere would be fine with him, just as long as it wasn't Bleddington.

The downstairs library was the smaller of the two within Hilltop Manor. Despite the upstairs library being larger and less confined, he hadn't stepped foot inside it since 1960. Not since his father had jumped through its stained-glass window, and to his death. At least, that's what the authorities had decreed had happened.

Royston closely guarded the truth, however.

His father didn't commit suicide, he was murdered. Yet, he didn't dare share his knowledge with the officials. If he did, he would be opening up a Pandora's box of further questions about past events that had long been buried.

Besides, who would ever believe him that the murderer was a young girl who had been dead for thirty years?

The sound of Mrs Weyland manoeuvring the Electrolux vacuum cleaner back and forth in one of the rooms upstairs travelled downwards. Hearing the droning white noise of the suctioning may have been an irritation to others, but to him it brought comfort. He didn't want to be alone right now.

As he opened the door to the downstairs library, his eyes were immediately drawn to the red carpet floor, and the set of wet, mud-stained footprints upon them. From the size of the shoeprints, he figured they belonged to a child.

"Willard," he sighed with disapproval, believing the muddy stains to have been caused by his son.

He must have come back home from school to fetch a book of some description for one of his lessons, he thought. It wasn't an unreasonable notion as there were a substantial number of reference books in the collection, many of them superior to what the school had to offer.

As he further examined the prints though, a cold shudder befell his soul. The shoe size of these tracks was too small to belong to Willard. He was a size eight, the same as himself. These tracks were smaller, size five, maybe a six.

"Mrs Weyland!" he bellowed as loud as he felt able to muster, whilst retreating from the room with haste. The volume at which he yelled only served to punctuate the fear in his voice.

No answer was forthcoming from the cleaner. The sound of the vacuum, coupled with her being on the higher floor level meant she couldn't hear her name screamed out.

Royston was relieved, at least it presented an opportunity to compose himself before trying to summon her attention again. There could still be a rational explanation for whom these footprints belonged to.

Royston made his way up the spiral staircase to speak to Mrs Weyland, feeling a sense of comfort in going to her, like a frightened child seeking refuge in their parent's arms after a bad dream. He wouldn't be so dramatic in claiming a reassuring embrace from her, just being in her company for a few moments would suffice.

It was Mrs Weyland's turn to be startled as the sound of her employer's voice came from behind, loud enough this time to overwhelm the vacuum's monotonous drone.

"Holey Moley, Mr Jennings, you gave this old girl a fright. Is everything ok?"

"Everything's fine," he lied. "Has anyone been here today?"

"No one," the response came. "Why? Are you expecting someone?" she asked with quiet optimism, hoping that some company other than his son or herself was on the horizon for this lonely soul.

"No," he lied again. "Thank you, Mrs Weyland. For everything."

He made his way with trepidation back down the staircase. His instinct should have been to run. Run far away from this house. Run far away from this town. Yet, he knew that wasn't a feasible option. Others before him had tried leaving and running from her, and all they had achieved was a faster, more vengeful demise.

Royston returned to the library carrying a basin of soapy water and a sponge. He didn't want Mrs Weyland to notice the mess. He didn't want her asking any questions about where they had come from. He didn't want to bring her into any harm's way.

As he laid eyes upon the carpet again though, no footprints could be seen. It was as if they had never been there.

# 10

School had finished for the day and, after walking with Tommy and Drake to their homes, Willard made his way up the steps to Hilltop Manor as fast as he could muster, with the intention of interrogating his father over any knowledge he may have had over what used to be the annual Halloween parties.

Even had he not been in such a rush to work on his assignment, the developing signs of an inferior sequel to the previous night's box-office rainstorm were making their presence known. The first splattering of drops had already taunted Willard by landing with a sporadic teasing upon him.

Had Mrs Weyland still been there, he would have much preferred to ask her about the news article instead. She would certainly have been more welcoming to a conversation than his father was. She was old enough to have remembered, or at least have knowledge of the parties. Maybe, she knew why and when they ended.

This was all a moot point for Willard, however. She would have finished her work by now and wouldn't be due back for another two days. His father would have to suffice.

To say Willard's relationship with his father was a cold one would be putting it politely. He wouldn't call it strained per se, mainly because they had never pulled at it hard enough for it to become so. It was merely an odd relationship which had long ago been accepted for being what it was. An expected distance between them had been there ever since he was old enough to hold a memory.

Although Willard was no therapist, and, by God, he was certain he would need one by the time he was older, his working theory was that his father held a deep resentment towards him for his mother's death during childbirth.

'If you had never been born, your mother would still be alive,' he envisaged his father thinking, though had never said it out aloud - at least, not to him anyhow.

Willard searched the mansion for his father and couldn't help but ponder that, in a parallel universe, his childhood would have been the happiest ever, and searching for his father in this giant house was the latest leg in an ongoing series of the greatest game of hide and seek there had been.

The sad reality was, however, there had never been any games in this house during his tenure. Toys, sure, an abundance of them. His father's wealth saw to that. But games - with other people - nothing.

Even his best friends weren't permitted to enter the home. He had an inkling this was why they always insisted on meeting him at the foot of the hill, to compensate for them never being able to be with him when he needed to see their smiles and hear their laughs the most.

As he dwelled on the lack of laughter and interactions inside the house, he pondered if this was the reason he had been so drawn in by the article about his grandfather's parties for the townsfolk - a surrogate feeling of participation and acceptance that had never been experienced by himself.

But, again, he was no therapist.

Instead, as he skulked up the cast iron, coal-black, spiral staircase, he found this would-be game of hide and seek was nothing but a joyless chore. A part of him thought of discarding the whole notion of writing about the parties and knocking up something for the fallback story about the near-fatal mining accident instead. It wasn't as though he wouldn't be able to do a capable job of it.

He ambled along the upstairs West Wing corridor, and his eyes were drawn to an ajar door to the room at the end of the landing. The upstairs library.

Willard picked up his lethargic pace and bounded towards the open door. The mere fact it was unlocked was a momentous occasion. For as long as he'd held a memory, he had never known it to ever be anything but so.

It was one of only two rooms within the house that had been permanently locked, the other being the sitting room where his mother had passed away during his birth.

The only reason he even knew there was a library upstairs in the first place was because his father and Mrs Weyland always referred to the downstairs library as, well...the downstairs library. By Willard's sound logic, if there was a downstairs library, there must be an upstairs one too. And the reason it had been locked, his sound logic continued, was because that was the room where his grandfather had killed himself.

When he was younger, Willard had once asked Mrs Weyland if she knew his grandfather at all. In reply, she innocently let slip that his grandfather had killed himself several years before she'd started cleaning here.

No sooner than those words escaped her mouth, and she had seen the mortified look upon the six-year-old child, she'd realised what she had done. The look of horror on her face almost rivalled the boy.

She'd come close to losing her job over that incident, more so since it had forced Royston to show rare compassion and tenderness to his son for a few weeks as the nightmares of his grandfather killing himself in a variety of ways plagued his young mind.

Willard entered the library and saw the boarded window. The memories of his nightmares came flooding back. Although the method of his grandfather's suicide had never been disclosed to him, seeing the thick planks of wood across the pane filled in the obvious blanks.
Yet, something more was at play here, he was sure of it.

The upstairs library was the last room along the left-hand side of the corridor and, as such, the window was facing the town from atop the hill he had travelled up and down far too many times. He knew the face of the house intricately, every detail, every blemish - and the impressive stained-glass window to this room was far from a blemish. It was not only unspoiled but also a finely detailed portrait of the town's tin mine.

Willard felt overcome with stupidity. How had he not thought of it before? The stained glass was not a part of the original house.

Hilltop Manor had been built in 1830 AD, and the tin mine, in the form it was depicted in the glass, wasn't founded until 1890. So why were boards covering the inside of the perfectly fine window on the upper floor? It appeared as if they were there to stop someone from jumping out again.

Willard surveyed the rest of the library and passed eyes upon the collection of books within the towering regiment of bookcases standing tall throughout the room and against the walls.

Until now, he had always thought the downstairs library to be the finest he had ever stepped in. Granted, his only other points of reference had been the Bleddington town library and the school library, so the bar had been set pretty low.

The downstairs library already felt inferior in every conceivable way. The size of the room, the volume of books, the variety of said books, the furniture - even the musky smell was more impressive. The boy had now found yet another reason for resentment towards his father, this time for keeping this wonderful room from him.

Then, he noticed the mask resting upon the centre of a reading table he had already glanced over. It was a vibrant red, plastic, devil's mask, complete with horns, a goatee beard made of what he hoped to be animal hair, and a malevolent smile. He had put missing this mask on his initial viewing of the table down to the over-stimulation hindering his senses at seeing the room for the first time.

Willard walked over to the mask and lifted it from the surface. The thoughts of trying it on for size had crossed his mind for a moment, yet he soon thought better of the foolish notion. He had read the books of M.R James, E.H Benson, and Sheridan Le Fanu in the downstairs library, so knew nothing good ever came of adopting a mysterious object. Nonetheless, he carried the mask with him in his hand, forgetting to put it back down as he continued to explore the texts upon the spines of the books in greater detail.

An angry and booming voice came from behind, startling him.

"What are you doing in here?" his father bellowed with venom.

There had been few times since he was a child where his father had lost his temper with him and, looking back, there was no doubt he had deserved the berating. Yet, as he saw the flustered face coupled with the wild look in his father's eyes, he was certain this time his wrath was unjustified.

The look of anger soon turned to one of panic though. His eyes caught sight of the red mask still within his son's right hand.

"Where did you get that?" he yelled.

"I found it, on the reading table," the intimidated reply came.

"Impossible," were the words he wanted to exclaim, yet he refrained from saying such declarations aloud. He didn't want his son asking any questions. Still, this single word echoed relentlessly in his stuttering thoughts. Impossible.

It had belonged to Huxley Finch, and they had all made sure they disposed of their masks on that night, all those years ago.

"Get out," he commanded with authority once he had composed himself. "If I ever see you in this room again, I'll be giving you one lashing of my belt for every year of your age. You hear?"

Willard did hear. He scurried out of the room fighting back the tears that came from his seldom-experienced berating. As much as he longed to look back at the upstairs library for one last time, he didn't want to lay further eyes upon his father.

He heard the door slam hard behind him, and a key wrestling with the lock.

Despite the hour only being late afternoon, Willard retreated to his bedroom and didn't leave it for the rest of the day. Any hopes he had of asking his father about the parties that used to happen here had gone. For now.

# OCTOBER 29, 1985

# 1

Willard awoke with a shiver.

With the manor as old and as large as it was, along with the added altitude of being situated on top of the hill, the bitterness of the Autumn morning was inevitable.

This morning felt colder than usual.

The bedroom was still shrouded in feint darkness, yet enough light from the burgeoning dawn infiltrated the curtains. He was able to make out the time on the wall clock without too much strain.

07:10.

Willard scraped with his fingers some of the crusted sleep from his eyes and took a look over to the bedside table where an exercise book, littered with barely legible notes and scribbles, remained open on top of the Gazette. He must have fallen asleep whilst working on the assignment. He had been so tired and drained, he couldn't remember for certain what he had written. He suspected it would be a struggle for him to salvage whatever hadn't been crossed out to make into a coherent story.

Then, a familiar sound of sobbing came.

In the corner of the room, the spectre of the girl with a porcelain face was hiding in the shadows.

'No, not hiding. That would be the wrong phrase,' Willard thought to himself. Hiding would suggest she didn't want to be noticed. The sudden and penetrating sound of the figure's cries indicated she yearned to be seen and heard.

Willard realised now, she hadn't been the nightmare he convinced himself it was.

The boy opened his mouth to speak, to plead with her what she wanted from him, but all that escaped was a vapour trail of his cold, winter breath.

The twisted figure stepped forward.

The sound of limbs snapping was more sickening than what he remembered, what he had tried to block from his memory.

She took a couple of small steps and stopped. Any reprieve from the cracking sound of bone he hoped for was not forthcoming.

She raised her arm and pointed at him.

The thick, red, coat she wore wasn't enough to hide that her crooked arm had been broken in multiple places. The uneven, bulging, fabric of the coat from where the protruding bones had been poking underneath nauseated Willard.

She commenced with one more step.

The teenager bolted from his bed in fear and retreated from his room with haste.

# 2

Willard didn't even wash or brush his teeth before making his rapid evacuation from Hilltop Manor.

So what, if he was going to smell a bit unsavoury for the day. It was a preferable option to being terrorised by a freaky ghost in his bedroom.

At least there was a corner shop en route to school, which stocked an excessive amount of Trebor mints. This was most likely to counter the excessive packs of cigarettes it also sold, to an excessive number of kids. As for the deodorant, Insignia was the corner shop's aerosol of choice. A cheap but not-so-cheerful shower in a can which made your armpits feel like they'd been napalmed in the morning, and you didn't love the smell.

Luckily, if he could categorise himself being lucky as the right term, Willard had clean underwear and a school uniform in the ironing basket in the downstairs utility room. Mrs Weyland had put them all in to wash and dry when she had cleaned his bedding. As for his bag, he'd dumped that at the foot of the coat stand in the hall the afternoon before, upon returning to, what he could now refer to with legitimacy, his haunted house.

He had everything he needed to make his sharp exit. He'd skipped breakfast in the dining room, but he was certain his father wouldn't mind. Willard was sure he'd still be pissed at him over the upstairs library incident.

The more he thought on it now, the more he was convinced the girl with a porcelain face was responsible for unlocking the room. But why would she want to show him the mask, and the means of his grandfather's death?

Willard made his way down the steps of the hill. He took a glance at his digital Casio watch. He was almost an hour earlier than when he would tend to leave.

Despite the cold October weather, he resolved to himself he wouldn't go back inside any time soon, not until he had a better understanding of what the hell was going on.

Forever the optimist, at least now one of the minor questions, which had been burrowing at the rear of more pressing thoughts, was able to be answered. He would finally know what time his friends would show up to needlessly wait for him, since they had always been there, without fail, when he got to the foot of the hill.

As he got closer to the base, it wasn't the two figures of Tommy and Drake he observed waiting for him, but a solitary, taller person. It took him several more steps before he recognised it as Nathanial Finch.

So much for the idea of not returning to the house, Willard thought to himself as he weighed in his mind what was the lesser of two evils, the ghost, or the bully?

Still, he continued his descent. As far as he figured, Finch had no beef with him, and if he had been there to ambush Drake for yesterday's insurgency, then he would surely have chosen a better spot to do so.

"Jennings!" Finch called out once their eyeline officially met. His tone wasn't threatening or demanding. If anything, he was hesitant and nervous. Understandable given the loss he had endured.

"Finch!" Willard called back. "Is everything okay?" He regretted in an instant the banality of the question. Of course, he wasn't okay. His entire world had been shaken.

"Well, aside from losing my father yesterday, everything is hunky-dory." The loud response came. "I mean, I've inherited enough money to set me up for life. I'm not going to get hit about stupid anymore by that asshole any

49

time I do or say something that rubs him the wrong way. Plus, I'm probably going to be rehomed away from this shithole town. What's not to love about life right now? Every cloud, right?"

Finch paused for a while and looked towards the darkening sky.

"Even clouds with silver linings still turn black and shower shit upon you though it would seem."

Willard said nothing. Not because he didn't want to, but because he didn't know how.

Thankfully, Finch would prove to be a more accomplished instigator of conversation.

"I bet you're wondering what I'm doing here," he spoke, pulling out a pack of Lambert and Butler cigarettes from his thick, olive-green winter jacket. "Do you smoke?" he asked, offering the pack.

Willard shook his head to say he didn't.

Finch let out a wry smile, suggesting he figured as much, before taking one for himself and lighting it.

"What are you doing here?" Willard asked.

"I thought you'd never ask," the sarcastic response came. Finch looked upwards toward Hilltop Manor. "Nice digs you got. My father used to hang out here loads when he was my age. Your dad and mine were pretty tight once upon a time, or so I've been led to believe. I always figured they'd have tried to make us hang out and force a friendship upon us or something. But, if anything, he always seemed dead set against it for some reason. Yet here we both are."

Finch put the cigarette to his mouth. Willard couldn't help but notice his hand was trembling, and he had a sense it had little to do with the cold crisp air.

He lit the cigarette and took a deep breath upon it to calm him, like an asthmatic taking in from a pump. Once composed, he blurted out a sentence that shook Willard.

"Do you know anything about a girl with a porcelain face?"

Willard guessed his reaction to the question must have been a sight to behold as Finch looked even more graven from noting his response.

"I'll take that as a yes," the uneven retort came as Finch took another deep drag of the cigarette.

"You've seen her too?" Willard asked. He didn't care how dumb he sounded now, there were already too many other thoughts which needed digesting.

"Yeah, I've seen her alright, almost a week ago now. At first, I'd managed to convince myself it had been nothing but a nightmare."

Willard nodded, he empathised with that rationale only too well.

Finch continued.

"That was, at least, until I told my father about it. I don't even know why I told him in the first place. I wouldn't exactly say we had the kind of relationship where we exchanged dream journals. All I knew is that I just had to get off my chest what I'd dreamt...what I'd seen.

I immediately wished I hadn't. He seriously lost his shit with me. I mean, I've never seen him flip out so much before in my life, and believe me when I say, he's flipped out a lot. Never like this though. This time was different. He wasn't losing his shit because he was pissed at me, he was losing his shit because he was scared, like truly scared.

Anyways, fucked-up long story made fucked-up short. It turns out, after telling him about the girl with a porcelain face, he went to visit his solicitor to update his last will and testament. He also handed the solicitor a sealed envelope with the orders of giving it to me, on the event of his death.

What happened to my father yesterday had something to do with the girl with a porcelain face, I'm sure of it. Multiple eye-witness statements said he was backing away scared from someone, but they said no one was there. I think there was."

Willard couldn't help but notice the ashen look draining Finch's face as he took one last heavy draw upon the cigarette before tossing it to the ground and extinguishing it with his Doc Martin boot.

"How did you know I'd seen her too?" Willard suddenly thought to ask. "I mean, I guess you're not going around door to door asking people if you've seen...well...whatever it is we've seen."

"The envelope. I think, it was my father's messed up way of saying I needed to reach out to you."

Finch swung his backpack around from off his shoulder and proceeded to unzip it. He pulled out what looked to be a photograph. Willard could only see the blank white rear of the photo for now, and some handwriting upon it, though he wasn't quite close enough to read what it said. He didn't have to wait long to be filled in, however, as Finch's still-trembling hand passed it over to his.

*To, Nathanial.*

*The sins of the father are to be laid upon the children.*
*Beware the girl with a porcelain face.*

"What do you think it means?" Willard spoke.

"I think it means whatever beef that china-faced bitch had with my dad, she now has with me too. That's just typical of my asshole father. He leaves me a large inheritance with one hand and a vengeful spirit with the other.

Check the date on the photo," Finch continued.

Willard looked at the rear of the photo. It read,

*October 31st, 1955.*

He threw a confused look over to Finch that implied the date meant nothing to him. Finch rolled his eyes with frustration.

"The other date, numbnuts."

Willard looked again but couldn't see any other date, much to the frustration of his companion. Then the realisation dawned upon him. From where he had been holding the photograph with his finger and thumb, he had been obscuring the second date. As he shifted hands, the same handwriting presented itself.

*October 28th, 1985*

"That's yesterday," he exclaimed.

"Which, says to me, my father knew when he was going to die. Turn the photo over."

Willard complied. So transfixed was he with what he had been hearing, he had foregone all instincts to look at the image on the other side.

The photograph was a black and white one. He assumed that the date on the bottom left corner had been the date it was taken.

There were eight men in the picture. A row of four middle-aged men standing behind four teenage males sitting down. Hilltop Manor was prominent in the background. He recognised most of the men instantly. Two of which stood out to him more than the others. His grandfather, Wilbur Jennings, stood behind his father.

"I think whatever your father was involved in, my father was too. Maybe, that's why we've both seen her," Willard speculated.

"Welcome to the vengeful spirit club," Finch attempted to joke, yet his attempts didn't register. Willard's attention had turned back towards the photograph. The other two men he recognised were Solomon Fisher and Huxley Finch.

"Is that your grandfather?" he asked, pointing to the man behind Huxley.

Finch nodded.

"Yeah, never met him though. He and my grandmother died in a fire before I was born. I'm guessing the person behind Solomon Fisher is his father too. I have no idea who the two people at the end are though. Any ideas?"

Willard shook his head.

"I don't, sorry."

"No worries. I have an appointment with Mr Fisher later this morning to talk funeral arrangements, I can ask him then. Speaking of which, I best be heading back home.

My father's cousin is staying over at my house until the courts decide what to do about me. She's nice enough, so I don't want to cause any extra stress for her by having her wonder where I am, and what mischief I'm up to. She's the only family I have left, I guess. My mum bolted on us, literally the day after I was born, taking a healthy chunk of cash from my father's bank account in the process, she's never been seen or heard of since. No loss.

I tell you what, I'll meet you at Lenchley Street Park after you finish school. Hopefully, we can make some more sense out of this...thing."

# 3

Royston peered into the dining room during his morning pilgrimage to the front door.

The relief overshadowed his guilt upon observing Willard's empty seat at the table. His sleepless night may have been embroiled by the nervousness over the inevitability of what was to come for him, yet it wasn't aided by the lousiness he endured for the tirade he lambasted to his son, for entering the upstairs library.

It hadn't been the boy's fault, and he decreed he would apologise to him. It didn't have to be a sweeping apology, nor was it to be overly heartfelt, but it was to be an apology, all the same, and that would suffice.

Royston proceeded to the hall, to retrieve the daily paper, which was always wedged, without fail, into the front door's letterbox.

He had left notes, along with several calls to the newsagents, politely requesting that the paperboy not leave the paper half stuck in the letterbox, as it meant the cold weather and stiffer winds, which came with being up on the hill, had easy access to the house - and the home was already chilly enough.

After several of these requests had been ignored, Royston started to think the defiance had been intentional. Maybe the paperboy's father had been one of the victims of the mine closure, and this was his means of cold-blooded, heartless, revenge - albeit a subtle and irritating one. If this was the case, he had all the makings of a criminal mastermind once graduating from being an earnest paperboy.

Royston emitted a frustrated sigh as he made a grab for the paper protruding from the letterbox. Then, in return, something made a grab for his throat.

He could feel the compression against his Adam's apple, applying the pressure. The attempts to draw breath were in vain as his windpipe became blocked by the unseen squeezing upon it.

He dropped to his knees as the strength oozed from his body, flashing flecks of white light began to appear in his vision as the oxygen became starved from his brain.

"This is how it ends," he couldn't help but think to himself.

The grip softened, then relinquished.

The heavy grasps for air were desperate and frantic as Royston devoured the air in an effort to replenish it inside his lungs. He looked around to see if he could lay his weakened eyes on his assailant. Yet he was alone. Royston forced himself back to his feet and staggered through the hall resembling someone who had partaken in far too many spirits, and not of the kind that was trying to kill him.

He'd made a few more steps. His breath had now returned closer to normal. Royston savoured each inhalation; it was as grateful an experience he had experienced for a long time. Then the strangling came again.

Royston performed an instinctive grab for his throat, to try and prise away the unseen hands clenched around it, yet the only hands upon his neck were his own.

He spun to face the hall's grand mirror, in order to face his assassin, yet the only reflection cast was of himself.

As he began to drift into unconsciousness, once more the invisible grip softened to allow him to breathe.

This same tortuous cycle would continue for another hour.

# 4

Finch's disappointment upon opening the door and seeing Ben Kruss wasn't his anticipated response, given he should have been experiencing an overwhelming sense of grief at the appointment to arrange his father's funeral.

Yet, his mind had been far more focused on the prospect of interrogating Solomon Fisher about the two unknown people in the photograph he had been left.

Maybe, it had been his way of dealing with the grief, along with his hope of trying to make some sense of the unexplainable shit that was the girl with a porcelain face, and what it meant for Willard and himself.

It may even have been a subconscious yearning to learn more about his father's life from when he was a similar age.

Either way, he had been eager for Fisher's arrival. His understudy, Ben Kruss, did not fit into any of the plans he had prepared for. Finch begrudgingly gestured for him to go into the living room.

"I'm sorry for your loss, young Nathanial," Ben spoke incredulously, once he was seated inside the lounge.

"And I'm sorry that you sound like a bit of a prick," Finch's harsh and unprovoked rebuttal came.

He didn't mean what he said at all, it was merely the frustration of the moment coming out. He suspected Ben was as nice as they came, and despite his young years for the business he was in, he had a sincere and welcoming demeanour about him.

"Nathanial!" his father's cousin, Georgina, called out in dismay from her seat. "That's no way to speak to Mr Kruss. Apologise to him, right now."

Though he would never admit it aloud, he was grateful for her justified intervention. He wanted to apologise as soon as the words spat with venom from his mouth, yet his ego wouldn't allow him to of his own accord.

"I'm sorry," he mumbled. "It's just grief talking, and all that shit."

"That's quite all right, Nathanial," Ben spoke amiably, seeming genuinely unoffended. "I've had stranger responses during these most difficult of times. Believe it or not, I once had a widow flash her breasts at me when I asked about who was going to read the eulogy."

Ben glimpsed the slightest of smiles and a look of amazement appear on the teenager's face.

"Wow, for real?"

"For real," he confirmed, skilfully taking any awkwardness and hostility away from the boy.

"I bet you loved that," Finch questioned.

"Sadly not," the regretful response came. "She was eighty-two years old at the time."

Finch let out an inadvertent laugh in response, giving Ben the perfect moment to pull out the required paperwork.

*********

Once the business of the funeral arrangements had been completed, Finch pounced upon his window of opportunity to bring up the subject of Ben's employer, Solomon Fisher.

"I'd have thought Mr Fisher would have taken the lead on this appointment," he stated inquisitively. "What with him and my dad being close friends and all."

Ben returned a confused look.

"Sorry, Nathanial, I don't know much about that I'm afraid. If they were close, it must have been long before my time working for Mr Fisher. I've never heard him talk of your father in any of our conversations. That's not to say they weren't close, of course. It's just... now I come to think of it, I've never noticed him mention much of his younger days at all.

Truth is, Mr Fisher told me he had to go somewhere for the morning and handed over all his appointments to me before he scurried off."

"So, you don't know who this could be in the photograph?"

Finch handed over the photo he had inherited to the apprentice funeral director.

"Wow, won't you take a look at that!" Ben marvelled. "Mr Fisher must have just about still been a teenager in that photo. This couldn't have been taken much before his father's death. Nasty business. Gives me shivers just thinking about it."

Ben surveyed the intrigued look embroiled on Finch's face and realised he had said too much, especially given the circumstances of why he was there in the first place.

"My sincerest apologies, Nathanial. My mouth has been known to get ahead of my brain on occasion. I don't think this kind of talk is appropriate," he corrected.

"Less so than telling me an eighty-year-old woman flashed her tits at you?" the counterpoint came.

"Fair point," the undertaker conceded. The boy had a valid argument.

"I'm guessing it would have been a little over thirty years ago the, accident, happened. It was a couple of years before I was born, but I've been told the stories off enough different people, even ex-reporters for the Gazette, for there to be at least some validity to them.

Any way's, it was supposed to be a routine funeral, a simple church service over at St Peters, followed by a burial in the graveyard. As straightforward as they came, in theory.

Trouble was, Franklyn Fisher was nowhere to be found.

It was minutes before the service was due to begin and the mourners had started arriving and filling out the church. The hearse had pulled up from the funeral parlour with the coffin.

Solomon, who must have only been eighteen or nineteen at the time, had been shadowing his father, learning the business as part of his apprenticeship. The poor soul had no choice but to step up and take charge of the proceedings. He took over so seamlessly, his father's absence wasn't missed by anyone, not in the know.

The service was a short one. The departed didn't have much of a family, so the eulogy was brief, sandwiched between a couple of generic readings and two standard hymns before the coffin was lowered to the grave and covered up. As I said, as simple as they came.

Only, when young Solomon returned to the funeral parlour did he realise something was amiss. He was hoping his father would be there. Not so he could berate him for throwing him in at the deep end so unexpectedly, but to let him know how perfect the service had gone.

Solomon had assumed his father's nonappearance had been down to him hitting the bottle a bit more than he should have that day.

It had become no secret his drinking problem had advanced from excessive drinker to flourishing alcoholic. Many suspected that was why he had been riding his boy so hard in learning every detail of the business, so he could pick up the slack when he was otherwise incapacitated.

Solomon reasonably figured he had been sleeping off the drink somewhere.

When he noticed the black trousers and shoes sticking out underneath one of the tables in the cool room, where they kept the departed in their coffins, his first instinct was that his father had passed out there. As he got closer, however, his unease grew. He couldn't hear any snoring or breathing. The sense of dread that he wasn't unconscious at all, but worse, clouded over him.

Solomon's concerns soon turned to confusion. He was relieved to see the corpse wasn't his father, but instead, the body of whose service he'd just conducted.

His pride at the smoothness of his inaugural service soon turned into alarm at the thought he'd gone and buried the wrong corpse. Not only was there the bereaved to think of, but the fact he was facing a hellacious belting from his father for this colossal screw-up.

Whether it was foolishness, naivety, or fear of consequence that caused him to do what he did, who knows, but let's not forget, he was still little more than just a boy. Forgivable? Maybe not. Understandable? For sure.

He waited until nightfall, and with a couple of other employees he'd thrown some extra money to, they proceeded to dig up the coffin with the hope of switching bodies before anyone would ever learn any differently.

I can't pretend to imagine what went through Mr Fisher's mind when he flipped the lid and laid eyes upon his father's body. His fingers were a bloody, shredded, mess, and the nails were snapped away from where he had been trying to claw his way out of the coffin, the look of desperation and panic etched upon his face.

The inquiry's verdict was death by misadventure.

With the amount of alcohol in his system, it was believed he had taken it upon himself to sleep it off in the coffin and had removed the corpse to do so. I mean, it's far-fetched, but some people do stranger things under the influence of drink, that's for sure. He must have closed the lid on himself, and whoever grabbed the coffin to take it to the hearse, must not have noticed the body under the table. Either way, it sends chills.

If it's taught Solomon one thing, however, it's to always be as meticulous as possible over every single detail of a service."

Ben could see the look of amazement upon Finch's face. It far surpassed the look of when he was told about the breast-flashing incident. The look of disapproval from Finch's cousin surpassed even that.

"Do you know either of these two?" Finch asked pointing to the two individuals stood beside his father.

"Sorry, Nathanial, I can't say I do. As I said, this photo was taken long before I was born, and I can't recall ever seeing either of them around town."

The look of frustration at not getting the answer was clear on the boy's face, yet his talk with the undertaker's apprentice wasn't without benefit.

A worrying pattern was starting to form. Out of the four elder people in the photograph, three of them he knew to be dead. All of them had been through far-from-natural causes, and the fourth was whereabouts unknown.

Now, it would seem his father was continuing that trend for the next generation. The sins of the father are to be laid upon the children indeed.

# 5

"I had a hunch I'd find you here, old chum," a warm and familiar voice spoke from behind Royston.

The cemetery of St Peters may have been located at the rear of the church, but annexed to the side of the chapel was a smaller, more discrete, graveyard - no more than eighty metres squared.

The private family plot had been gifted to Hector Jennings over a century earlier, in exchange for a healthy Christian donation to the church for its much-needed renovation.

Royston had been busying himself alternating his perturbed glances between the gravestone of his father, and the mocking empty space next to it.

"Checking out your new home?" Solomon spoke with inappropriate impishness.

Royston turned to face his old friend. The bloodshot eyes and heavy baggage underscoring them were enough of a sight to trick Sol into thinking he'd momentarily wandered onto the set of Bleddington's own remake of the Night of the Living Dead.

"Jesus Christ!" Solomon declared, before remembering his surroundings. "Oh, shit. Can I say that here?" He made the sign of the cross in a tongue-in-cheek manner and mouthed the word, 'sorry' to the air. "Bad dreams?"

"You've got to be able to sleep in order to have bad dreams. What are you doing here?" Royston asked without enthusiasm. He wasn't in the mood for his friend's misguided sprightliness this morning.

"Visiting my dear old pappa and cursing the moment he talked us into covering up what happened that night. You?"

"Pretty much the same."

"You've seen her, haven't you?" Sol questioned further. His perpetual sprightliness was on pause for now.

Royston pulled at his collar to display the small hand marks embedded into his neck.

"You could say that."

"Jes..." Sol went to say again but refrained himself from besmirching such a sacred place. "Fucking hell," he spoke instead. "She's really got it in for you, hasn't she, pal."

Royston proceeded to remove the brown leather satchel that had been over his shoulder and let it dangle in his right hand by his side. With his free left hand, he gestured to the wooden bench that was standing against the stone wall of the secluded place of rest. The two friends sat.

Sol gazed at the gold plaque fixed to the middle of the top panel. It read,

**Kindly Donated by Wilbur Jennings 1935**
**A friend to St Peters, and the town of Bleddington.**

"You know what," Sol declared, the perkiness was returning to his tone after the briefest of hiatuses. "I should donate a bench too. Not one as fine as this though. I'm thinking, maybe, a shoddily made one, with lots of splinters and stray nails sticking out of the seat. That way I still get to be a pain in the ass to the people in this town, even long after I'm gone."

Royston couldn't help but let out a little laugh upon hearing this. The mirth wasn't destined to last.

"She left me this yesterday."

Royston reached into the satchel and pulled out the red devil mask.

"Oh," was Sol's short but subdued response. "We don't have long left, do we?"

"I fear not."

The two sat in silence for a while, comfortable in the other's company, as they always had been. The silence was broken by a statement Sol had not expected to hear from his friend.

"You've probably joined the rest of the town at some point, in wondering why I closed down the mine so abruptly."

"To be honest, I'm one of a very finite number who didn't. Well, not at first, anyway.

I thought I knew better than anyone what was going through that noggin of yours. Not that I'd ever share your thoughts with anyone else, of course. Partly through the sheer reason that it's none of their bloody business, but also because of the consequences doing so might bring.

At first, I'd put it down to you wanting to make the most of what life you have left, as best as you could, without the extra stress or burden that running an operation as big as that brings. But the more I thought about it, the more I realised that I was barking up the wrong tree. You wouldn't have put that many people out of work for your own gain.

The people of this town may curse you for being a heartless bastard, but they don't know you like I do. I know for a fact you're a bastard, but you sure aren't a heartless one. You could have easily hired someone to take on the day-to-day logistics of the mine, kept everyone in work, and still reaped the rewards of everyone else's efforts in the meantime. That's one of the many privileges of being rich, is it not?"

"It was because of a vision I had," Royston clarified. "More than just a vision though. A premonition. And a chilling one at that.

In my vision, there was a disaster in the mine. A big one. A shaft had collapsed, and a substantial number of miners didn't make it out alive. It wasn't an accident, though. Through the darkness of the pit, I could see the porcelain mask, watching as they perished. It got me thinking. What if, after she's done with us, her spirit still endures? If retribution is all that it's ever known, what if it doesn't want to rest once it's vengeance has been served?

No one could deny we deserve what's coming to us, but the rest of this town sure doesn't. The townsfolk may despise me for ending many of their livelihoods, and that's my burden to bear, I'm thick-skinned enough to take their resent. But what they don't know is that I'm trying to save their lives too, and that is my last chance for penance."

"Jesus Roy," Sol grimaced again and once more apologised to the heavens and made the sign of the cross. "Have you ever thought though, that maybe it wasn't a premonition at all?

Maybe, and hear me out on this radical train of thought, just maybe, it was nothing more than a dream. I've dreamt all kinds of dark shit after what happened with my father, but that's all they were, simple dreams, brought on by all the guilt and grief we've had to live with over the years."

"Maybe," Royston conceded. "But it's not the first time I've had a vision like this come to pass as true.

Long before Willard was even conceived, I had a dream about the death of his mother during his birth. I mean, it was so vivid, it put me off the prospect of us trying for children.

I didn't say any of this to Constance of course. How could I?

Whenever she brought the idea up of starting a family in conversation, I just tried changing the subject as best I could. Christ." It was now Royston's turn to apologise to the heavens and mime the cross. "I even had a vasectomy without her knowledge, with the intention of telling her things just weren't to be when we couldn't conceive.

But she got pregnant anyway. A part of me wished it was infidelity, and the kid wasn't mine. Perhaps then they would both stand a chance of staying away from, her, wrath. But, by all accounts, these procedures are never guaranteed. Besides, I knew she would never do that to me. The kid was mine, no doubt about it.

I tried doing the best I could to persuade myself that it was just a silly dream, a result of guilt and grief, just as you said. But there was just something so malevolent about it.

When, it, happened, I felt like I was replaying the same videotape all over again. Everything was identical. Almost.

I was called home from the office by the midwife. I'd insisted on a hospital birth, not because I particularly felt strongly about it, I was just trying to find ways to ensure things would happen differently to what I'd seen.

It was clear from the midwife's unscheduled call, however, that the birth was going to have to take place at our home. My only solace had been that the midwife had assured me, aside from the labour happening earlier than planned, everything was otherwise going smoothly. Only when I showed up back home did things start to go south.

Constance started to panic, and the seizures began. The midwife said it may have been a convulsive syncope, a seizure-like episode caused by an irregular heartbeat. She had to get the baby out straight away.

My wife didn't survive, exactly as I had foreseen."

Royston saw by the sorrow on Sol's face that the story had shaken him. Seldom was he lost for words, yet this was one of those dates and times to mark in the diary. Eventually, he spoke.

"You made a point of saying the dream was almost identical. What was different about it?"

"The spirit was visible to me in the vision, yet I couldn't see her in the sitting room where the birth was taking place.

Constance could see her though. Nothing else could have caused her to panic so much.

In the vision, she was by Constance's side, staring at her with those empty eyes. If we can even call them eyes.

I don't know what she saw in the void behind the mask, and it would break my heart and drive me to the brink of insanity in the process even trying to think. All I know is that it was enough to cause a healthy thirty-year-old woman to have a heart attack.

That's not the worst of it either. In the vision, after the midwife had managed to save Willard, the way the spirit focused her attention upon him, I could tell she had intentions for the boy.

Once he was born, I made a promise to myself that I wouldn't let myself bond with him.

It may sound selfish, and it probably is, but I was trying to soften the emotional blow for when the inevitable happens.

If she gets me first, then I'm hoping that Willard resents me enough not to grieve as hard as someone who idolised their father, as much as I did. And, if that bitch is cruel enough to take his young life before she takes mine, well, I've been mourning him ever since the day he was born."

# 6

It wasn't unusual for Willard to be in such a rush to leave the classroom as soon as the welcoming sound of the buzzer rang, signifying the final class of the school day had finished. Almost every pupil shared with him the same zeal to escape. The buzzer may as well have been a starting pistol for chaos as the teachers' calls for calm to exit the classroom in an orderly fashion fell en masse against ignorant ears.

On this occasion, however, Willard exited amongst the scurrying swarm with a different kind of intent.

He had succeeded in making it as far as the school gates before a familiar voice called from behind.

"Hey, Will!" Drake projected. It may not have been a piercing yell, but it still made him cringe upon hearing it.

He turned around to see Drake and Tommy, flush in the faces from their efforts to catch up to him throughout the horde.

It was now Willard's turn to go red in the face - though this was from awkward embarrassment. He always walked home with them, it was as much of a ritual and unspoken expectation as them going to school together.

He'd already felt rotten enough for attempting to leave the school grounds without the courtesy of informing them he wasn't going to walk with them, and he felt even lousier about who it was he was ditching them for. If he'd told them that part, however, there would have been the inevitable questions, and Willard didn't want to start lying to his closest friends…his only friends.

"What the hell man!" Tommy rebuked. "What's the hurry dude? We always leave school together. Is everything okay?"

Willard was trying desperately to think on his feet for an answer which couldn't be construed as a lie, yet fortune was on his side. It was Drake who made the inadvertent untruth on his behalf.

"Holy shit, you're meeting a girl, aren't you?"

All Willard had to do was stay silent and look coy. Technically, it wouldn't be lying if he didn't say anything.

"Yeah, you are," Drake continued his awry assumption with pride. "Our boy's got himself a girlfriend."

"More like a Yoko?" Tommy contributed. The bitterness was still present in his voice. He clearly wasn't as forgiving of their friend bailing out on them without a word as Drake was. "The first time he's ever laid hands on a female that doesn't contain risks of paper cuts, and he's sneaking off like Lord Sneaky of Sneakyville. Population, one sneaky little prick."

"Ok guys, bust my balls all you like tomorrow, but I honestly do have to shoot."

"Of course you do, lover boy," Drake laughed.

Willard said nothing, he simply left and carried on walking with the same urgency. He didn't dare to keep Finch waiting.

*********

Finch cut a solitary figure as he sat on one of the swings contained within the playground off Lenchley Street. If it wasn't for the olive-green winter jacket he'd recognised from their earlier liaison, Willard would have been forgiven for thinking it was some creepy old man in the park instead.

In Finch's right hand, there looked to be a cigar, and not one of those Hamlets advertised on TV, but a big one. The kind sported by Hannibal in the A-Team.

"Jennings," he called out upon spotting Willard's approach.

Willard sat on the adjacent swing seat.

The smoke attracted to him like a magnet, slinking its way to his nostrils. He was undecided on whether he liked the aroma or not, yet he still emitted a cough as a trail invaded his sinuses. This caused a slight smile to appear on Finch's face.

"The cigars were my fathers," he explained. "I found a box of them in the kitchen earlier. They weren't left to me in the will, but I think they're fair game, don't you? I also came across a bottle of cognac I'll be claiming as my birth right too. Do you think the cigar makes me look cool?" he probed.

"They make you look about fifty," Willard's instinctive response came. He regretted his retort to the bully as soon as he spoke.

Finch let out a little laugh, however, and tossed the remnants of the cigar.

"So," Willard spoke. "Did you get anywhere with Solomon Fisher?"

"Nope, the scrotum pole didn't even show. Apparently, he had shit to do, so he sent his assistant instead."

"Well, if he won't come to us, maybe we could go to him. He lives at the funeral home, right? why don't we try him there? Tell him you've come to visit your father's body or something. He'd have to let you in for that, surely."

Willard felt lousy for suggesting he use his deceased father as an excuse, yet Finch didn't appear to mind so much. If anything, he seemed keen on the idea.

"Okay, Jennings, that sounds far more preferable than freezing my sack off on a kid's swing. His assistant only seemed to suggest he was due out for the morning. With a bit of luck, he should be back by now. Besides, I've got a messed-up story to tell you on the way about how his father died. If the girl with a porcelain face had anything to do with it, then holy shit, that's one pissed-off phantom. You better hope your dad's got some vengeful spirit cover on his life insurance."

# 7

No answer was forthcoming to the boys' heavy-handed round of doorbell ringing, nor to the even heavier flurry of knocking with their clenched hands. Upon trying the door handle it was evident it had been locked.

"Looks like no one's here either," Willard spoke. "He must still be out."

"A minor technicality," Finch commented. "You've heard the saying, where there's a will there's a way, right?"

Willard nodded his head wearily. He didn't like where this conversation was heading.

"Well, there's a lesser-known saying. Where there's a back door to an empty home, there's a way too. We can take a look for ourselves to see if we can find any answers about the girl with a porcelain face."

# 8

The back entrance pitched to Willard wasn't exactly as advertised on the tin.

What Finch had failed to mention in his suggestion, was that trying the back door also entailed scaling the large wall which separated the rear of the funeral home's grounds from the alleyway behind it - complete with the thin layer of barbed wire atop.

"There's that plan gone too," Willard bemoaned unconvincingly, attempting to sound disappointed they wouldn't be committing any criminal acts of trespassing.

The look thrown at him in return was one that reminded Willard of why he feared him. Their alliance may have been one born out of a mutual need for answers, yet he didn't think for one moment the school bully wouldn't turn on him on a flip of the coin, should he ever defy him.

"Don't you worry your saintly thoughts, my sweet little angel," Finch mocked dryly. "Only one of us will be able to get over. The other is going to have to stay here and stand guard like a good little soldier. What about it Private numbnuts, are you ready for guard duty?"

"What if you get caught inside?" Willard questioned further, aware he was starting to grate on his reluctant companion and test their forced coalition.

"I'll tell them it's all part of my grieving process. Give me your schoolbag," he ordered.

Willard may have been new to this trespassing game but, rather disconcertingly, he knew what Finch had in mind. He would use the backpack to shield himself from the barbed wire as he swung over the wall.

He handed the school bag to him and proceeded to assume the universal stance of, getting ready to give a 'leg up.'

"What the hell's going on, Will?" a voice called out from behind him. It was Drake. Inevitably, Tommy was by his side.

"What are you guys doing here?" Willard questioned.

"We've been following you since school finished. We wanted to see who the girl was you'd ditched us for, and unless our eyes deceive us, or she's had an extreme course of hormone replacement therapy, that's no girl."

Finch and Drake locked eyes, the disdain they held for each other was still palpable. The simmering stand-off between the two fledgeling foes was eased by Finch breaking into a smile of a sardonic nature.

"It's your lucky day," he proclaimed. "I have a job for you. Do it well and It'll be your stay of execution from me."

"Come on Drake," Tommy defied. "Let's leave them to it. Whatever Will has got planned with his new friend, it's not our problem."

"It's not like that, Tommy." Willard attempted to soothe.

"Then what is it, Will? As things look pretty damming from here."

"I can't explain it right now."

Tommy let out an exaggerated and frustrated sigh, before waving his hands dismissively.

"No, you don't understand," Willard proclaimed. "I don't even know how to explain what's happening right now. Something really messed up has been happening to us, like, quite literally, supernatural, messed up. I realise it sounds crazy, and a few times these past two days I've had to convince myself that I'm not, but you have to trust me on this. I swear it to you guys. I'll explain it all to you later, well, what I can explain."

Tommy stared at Willard for a few moments and concluded he was telling the truth, or at least he believed himself to be. He produced a frustrated sigh that was even louder than its predecessor.

"Okay, Will."

Finch let out a laugh before slapping Tommy across the back. It was as sarcastic a pat on the back as could be, and needlessly heavy-handed too.

"Looks like you are coming with me after all," he spoke to Willard. "Your two friends are on the lookout now."

# 9

The back door to the funeral parlour had been unlocked when they tested it.

This was both a relief and concern for Willard. Relief the potential felony of Breaking and Entering had been downgraded - it was now, merely Entering. And concern this was still a less harsh way of saying home invasion.

None of these worries appeared to register with Finch, however, at least not on his exterior. He was as cool as the proverbial cucumber.

Whether it was the strength of his conviction - a poor choice of word when committing a criminal act - or the confidence he held in his ability to talk his way out of any trouble they may find themselves in, he was grateful one of them possessed composure.

Upon pushing the door open, they were greeted by the sight of a couple of coffins resting on some heavy-duty trolleys. Finch even wondered for a prolonged moment if one of them belonged to his father. But then he remembered what Benjamin had told him on his earlier visit. His father was in the chapel of rest, which was located in the annex of the ground floor. These caskets, thankfully, were most likely empty – for now at least.

"Hello! Mr Fisher?" Finch called out, loud enough to merit an answer should he be inside.

A part of Willard wondered what his literal partner in crime was playing at, announcing their intrusion so brazenly, but as he proceeded, the method to his madness made itself clearer.

"Are you in? It's Nathanial Finch. We tried the front door and there was no answer. We were a bit concerned and are checking everything's ok?"

Clever lad, Willard thought to himself. If Mr Fisher was in, they would appear as good Samaritans as opposed to audacious trespassers.

No response was received to Finch's announcement.

"Looks like we've got the place to ourselves," Finch stated, "and we're not leaving here without answers, so we best be quick about this. Cover the front door in case he comes back. I'll do a quick recce and see if I can find anything that might give us some answers."

Willard nodded. He held no objection to this arrangement. Standing guard sounded more favourable than snooping around someone's personal belongings.

"If I find anything I'll shout for you," Finch commanded. Again, Willard nodded without much protest.

\*\*\*\*\*\*\*\*\*\*

Standing alone in the hallway, for what appeared substantially longer than his constant glances at his Casio watch informed him was little more than five minutes, allowed Willard ample time for some much-needed self-reflection.

Until three days earlier, he had considered himself the epitome of the worst category of teenager. Seldom in any trouble, hardly a daydreamer of any kind, and a mind which favoured practicality over imagination. He was even more occupied with his Commodore 64 than he was in chasing girls. He almost felt a traitor to his teenage kin.

Yet, like a werewolf changing at full moon, or Dr Jekyll turning into Mr Hyde, he believed he had transformed with little warning into a nefarious being with little semblance to his former self. Here he was, in the midst of a criminal act, due to the astounding belief he had been visited by a paranormal presence. My, how he missed being boring and unimaginative.

Then he heard Finch's yell.

It wasn't an excited call that suggested he had found the information they had been looking for. This was a frightened beckoning.

"Jennings!"

Willard ran to where the voice called from.

His initial thoughts were that Mr Fisher had indeed been in the parlour all along. He had caught Finch snooping through something he shouldn't have and was giving the boy a justified hiding.

He thought again. No, that couldn't be the reason. He suspected Finch had taken more than a few beatings from his father in his lifetime, a thrashing from someone else would be no different to someone singing a second-rate cover version of an overplayed song.

His voice called out again. Just as distraught as before.

He followed the voice to the annex, the place where the chapel of rest was located. The entrance door to the room was wide open.

He could see through the doorway the figure of Finch; his face was pale and shaken. The assured confidence and swagger of earlier had been scrubbed away.

Finch must have seen his companion's arrival through his peripheral vision as he acknowledged his presence by raising his arm and pointing.

Willard cautiously entered the room and took an instinctive look over to where Finch was directing. He too was certain he would have yelled in fear, had the breath not been sucked out of him by what he saw.

# 10

Two hours earlier.

Solomon Fisher was sat in the chapel of rest.

Usually, he avoided entering this room unless for the necessity of work.

It may not have been a religious room, yet he still considered it just as sacred. This place was the last real chance for the mourners to be with their departed before their final goodbyes at the funeral service, and today he felt justified in placing himself in their category instead of as an undertaker.

In his right hand was a bottle of cognac. In his left, a fine crystal highball glass. A matching glass was placed on top of the coffin in front of Solomon's chair.

"I know it's been a long time since we've drank together old pal, but if I remember correctly, this is your favourite brand. I went out and got a bottle special. If it's not your favourite, all I can do is apologise. Apologise for that, and a great deal of many other things," he addressed.

He poured a generous measure into the glass upon the coffin, then an equal measure into his own. He gently clinked the glasses and took a sip before taking a moment to savour the drink.

"You always did have finer tastes than the rest of us, Hux," Sol remarked. "Hah, the rest of us. That's a contradiction of terms if ever I heard one. It's only two of us left now. Royston, and myself. And I'm sure we'll be joining you very soon.

I would like to say, we'd be reuniting with you up there in heaven, as is the respectful, albeit cliched, thing to do. But you know me, I've always chosen to be honest over cliched. Honest over everything apart from the events of that night.

Truth is that chances are you're wallowing down in hell. I would say keep a seat warm for me, but, since it's hell, I'm making the assumption it's warm enough already. At least I'll be dressed for the occasion with my Hawaiian shirt when I get there."

He let out a little laugh to himself then followed it with an incongruous heavy sigh between taking a heavier sip.

"How did it ever come to this, Hux? All we had to do was the right thing by her. What happened may have been an accident to begin with but covering it up the way we all did made us all murderers, and every day we said nothing, it was like we were killing her all over again."

Sol clinked glasses.

"Until we meet soon, my old friend."

He downed the last of his drink as a shudder came over him. The sudden drop in the room's temperature could not be denied.

"I've been expecting you," he spoke with an unexpected calm.

Solomon stood from the chair and turned to face the spirit by the opposing wall of the chapel of rest.

He wasn't so assured as he had thought himself to be after all as he stared upon her. His legs almost gave in from under him. He placed a hand onto the chair for extra support.

The spirit's whimpering filled the quiet air as it made a pained step forward, the sound of cracking bone causing further unrest to Sol.

"I'm truly sorry for what happened to you," he spoke. "You've got to believe me when I say that."

She took another unnatural-looking step toward him.

"I always told myself, when this moment came, that when you'd come for me, I'd face my end with an acceptance and dignity, something we robbed you of the choice to do. You deserve your vengeance as much as I deserve your wrath."

She moved another step forward.

Sol's breaths became more rapid now.

"Here's the thing though. When I think about what you did to my father, and what you've done to my friends, I say dignity can go screw itself."

Sol reached into his trouser pocket and withdrew a pistol. He couldn't help but feel his hand trembling as he aimed the firearm at the figure. Her cries came louder now as she took another step closer.

Sol cocked the weapon. His unsteady hands were of no real consequence. She was close enough to him that it would be a remarkable feat not to strike her with a bullet. He attempted a deep and steadying breath and pulled the trigger.

The ammunition had no effect. The spirit didn't baulk as the projectile passed through her.

Another step.

He fired again. Higher this time, into that abomination she called a face.

Nothing.

She was just a few paces from reaching him. The weapon was of no use in stopping her.

Sol cocked the pistol once again, only this time he turned it on himself, pressing the barrel hard against his temple.

"My death is going to be at my hands, not yours."

He gave the figure a defiant smile before squeezing the trigger for one last time.

# 11

The look of shock upon Finch's face was the first thing that rattled Willard.

Until now he had been the epitome of calmness, confident beyond his years. Yet, as he burst into the chapel of rest and saw him sobbing and shaking, he looked as frightened as a five-year-old child lost without their parents at a fun fair.

Willard's eyes turned to face where Finch was staring, and he too, began to tremble.

He had never seen a corpse before. To be more precise, he had never seen a corpse that had its brains blown out before.

Only after the initial shock of seeing Mr Fisher's body on the floor did Willard realise the bigger picture. Not just a picture in fact, but a tragic tapestry.

The casket behind the body, covered in thick blood, small fragments of skull, and clotted lumps of brain matter, contained Finch's father.

Willard doubted his companion had been to see his father's coffin since his death, but even if he had, to see it now, defiled in such a way, was certain to be beyond distressing.

"Nathanial!" he called, unaware he was using the same name and tone his father used when berating him.

Though unintentional, it was enough to bring him back to the here and now.

Willard surveyed the room, more out of necessity from avoiding staring at the body for any longer. As he gazed at the opposite direction to where the remains of Mr Fisher lay, his eyes became fixed upon the wall.

"Somebody else was here," he declared.

Finch now turned to face where he was looking. True enough, a couple of bullet holes were displayed on the wall.

"Either he's a lousy shot or they went straight through the target," Finch stated.

"The girl with a porcelain face!"

"What the hell is going on, Jennings?"

"I don't know, but we need to call the police. We can't just leave him here and wait for someone else to find him."

Finch nodded begrudgingly in agreement.

"Go grab your friends and head somewhere away from here. I'll phone the police and wait for them to arrive. We'd do more harm if both of us are here, and we start contradicting each other when they ask their questions. I'll use the story of me coming to visit my father's coffin, and when there was no answer, I took it upon myself to come in anyway. It should hold enough weight for them. Unlock the front door and go out that way."

Willard nodded.

"I'll give you a call later, Finch. Hey, are you going to be, ok?" he asked with kindness.

Finch embraced Willard in a tight hug in response to the question. It was an unexpected gesture, but one he was only too pleased to accept.

A sad sense then came over Willard. A feeling that this was perhaps one of the few occasions where someone appeared genuinely concerned about Finch. Perhaps they were becoming friends after all.

"I'll get by," his answer came as he fought the tears. "I always do."

# 12

Royston was sat in the downstairs library attempting in vain to read one of the novels within.

His mind was unable to focus on the text as his eyes gazed with futility upon the page. His waning attempts at concentration were thwarted definitively by the sound of a ringing throughout the house. It was the doorbell connected to the pull chord of the front door. One of the many Victorian features of this house that, despite the modern equivalent being far more proficient, and sympathetic to the ear, had never been upgraded.

There had been a collection of bells within the hall, each with a different function, such as the kitchen bell and the butler bell. But since no staff had occupied the house for a number of years, the only ringing noise he needed familiar himself with was that of the doorbell.

Such was the infrequency he received visitors to Hilltop Manor these days, even to hear this ring was a rare occurrence.

He forced his weary body up from the chair. He'd debated internally for a moment on whether he should ignore the sounds. Yet, he soon chose to answer. Whoever had come to the house, such was the labour of the ascent up the hill, the reason for their cause must have been of importance.

Royston made his way to the door and opened it. No one was present.

Perhaps a sudden and strong gust had blown the door pull with enough force to set off the bell. Perhaps, he thought, but without any conviction. He was surer that it was her.

That's when he saw it. Fixed to the weight of the gently rocking door pull was a hideous clown mask. He recognised it immediately. It had been the one Sol had worn on the night of her death.

A terrible cocktail of sadness and fear befell him. Sadness at the realisation she had gotten to Sol and was sending him notice of his demise, and fear that he was the last of them left. Her vengeance would not be long now.

# 13

"What the actual fuck with an extra side order of double fuck," Tommy's not-so-elegant response came once Willard had finished sharing the extended highlights of the events which had transpired since he had first seen the girl with a porcelain face.

They had been in Drake's bedroom when the bombshell had been dropped. Their host had been unusually quiet as he digested what had been said.

"Holy shit, has anyone got the phone number for Peter Venkman, or the blooming exorcist?" Tommy inquired, still aghast. He may have intended it to have been said tongue in cheek, yet his voice displayed evident signs of distress. "So, let me understand this right. This girl with a porcelain face has some vendetta against the people in Finch's photo?"

"It's looking that way. That's why we were trying to find out who those two other people were in the picture. I mean, if they're alive and well, it means, maybe, my father can find a way too. That's why we went to the funeral parlour, to get some answers from Mr Fisher."

"Have you tried, you know, talking to your father?" Drake finally contributed. "It's a crazy idea, but it might just work." He made no attempt to hide his sarcasm.

"You've got more chance of getting a conversation out of Helen Keller than my father. He won't engage with me on the best of days, and right now, these aren't even close to being the best of days.

Yesterday, he found me in the room where my grandfather committed suicide. Well, where I thought he had killed himself. Now, I'm almost certain the girl with a porcelain face had a hand in it.

My father lost his shit with me just for being in that room, if he finds out I've been digging up anything else, who knows how badly he'd react. I always knew there was something from his past he was hiding, and I think the girl in the porcelain mask is trying to tell me what it is."

"Women eh, always sending mixed signals," Tommy joked, eliciting a soft laugh from his two friends.

"This morning, when I saw her again, I thought she was pointing at me. But now I've had time to replay that moment in mind, I think she could have been pointing to my bedside table, and the Gazette on top of it. The one Mr Kready assigned to me. There was something in there about the Halloween parties that my grandfather used to throw in my home. I'm sure that's got something to do with it."

"Your father owns the archives of the Gazette, right?" Tommy directed at Drake.

"Yeah, but it's a sensitive subject for him. The Gazette was my mother's entire world, other than Dad and me, of course. I'm sure I've already told you before, she was the editor for it back in the day. It was her grandmother who started the Gazette, you know. I guess she saw it as her duty to carry on the family legacy.

After she died, that's when the paper died too. It stopped publication in 1976. That's how we have so many years' worth of copies. My great-grandmother would never throw her first printed copy out, and I guess my grandmother and mother followed suit with that trait.

If you ask me, my father would be only too pleased to get shot of them, 'they take too much space up in our attic,' he says. I don't think he'd ever bring himself to bin them or give them away though. I'm amazed he even gave Mr Kready his spares. It was such a big part of my mother's life, so to let them go would be the same as letting her go, I guess. You've seen the printing presses taking up most of our garage. Dad can't even get his own car in there.

"So, all we need to do is go up to your attic for a bit?" Willard continued to hound.

"Yeah, I guess. He wouldn't like the idea of us snooping around them though, in case we damage anything. But what he doesn't know won't hurt I suppose, and tonight's his dart's league, so he'll be out for most the night."

"Alright, we wait for him to go out, then we'll go up and see what we can find. I'll give Finch a call and tell him to come up too."

"Do you have to?" Drake sighed. It clearly wasn't sarcasm this time.

"He's with us whether you like it or not. He's got as much at stake in this as I do, and it's already too late for his father."

"I don't like it," Drake confirmed, but he didn't put up an argument. It was no secret that if their uneasy co-existence maintained a truce, it would be of benefit to him.

# 14

Royston entered the study on the upper floor of the west wing and made a beeline towards the liquor cabinet.

He unlocked it to reveal numerous bottles, the majority of which had still to be opened. From the impressive and expensive collection, he singled out a bottle of fine vintage scotch which had once belonged to his father. He saw no purpose in leaving it unopened now.

Royston had been keeping it for a special occasion, and what event would be more befitting than what he anticipated could be his final night on this earth?

Whatever she had planned for him, he hoped his intoxication would numb the emotional and physical retribution for what was in store.

He had only got as far as unscrewing the top when he heard a call from outside the room. It was a voice he recognised as belonging to his father.

"Help!"

He immediately recalled this word as being the last one he had listened to Wilbur Jennings speak before his death.

That night, Royston had been downstairs when the plea reverberated throughout the house.

He had been watching This Is Your Life on the black and white TV they had newly acquired, whilst his father had been in the upstairs library - feeding his brain instead of rotting it - as he liked to inform him.

Upon hearing the call that night, Royston scurried upstairs. The library door had been locked from the outside. 'How could it be?' he'd thought to himself.

From inside the room, the sound of glass breaking and a rapidly fading male scream was heard. Seconds later, the key twisted, unlocking the door, allowing it to swing open wide of its own accord, displaying a taunting view of the murder scene.

That was almost thirty years ago, and the thoughts of another trick being played on him by the girl with a porcelain face were overruled by the prospect of seeing his father once again, even if in spirit form. It would give him the chance to at least say goodbye and gain some closure.

He hastily exited the study and entered the corridor. The door to the neighbouring upstairs library was wide open, inviting him in. Daring him, to enter.

He obliged.

The planks of wood which had boarded up the library's stained-glass window had been prised away from the wall and discarded onto the floor, revealing the intact pane.

Royston took several steps further into the room. He may even have ventured a few more had it not been for the sudden and loud sound of the door slamming shut behind him. He spun round instinctively and made a grab for the handle. The door had been locked from the outside.

"Help!" his father's voice pleaded.

Royston turned again and could see his father. A terrified look was fixed upon Wilbur Jennings' face. Though it was he who was the ghost, the look disregarded his son as if he wasn't there.

"Dad!" Royston called out, yet his words went unheard.

Wilbur began to back away from something in the room through fear, the whimpering seeped through his gaping mouth as he displayed pleading looks to his assailant.

Royston couldn't help but note how weak his father looked, this man who was both venerated and feared throughout the town from his wealth and power was now begging like a coward.

He withdrew, closer to the window in retreat, until his back was against the pane. The sickening sound of the glass tantalisingly beginning to splinter, and crack, played as the figure of his father was pressed tight against the surface.

The signs of struggle were clear upon him, yet whatever was pushing him was too strong. The spirit of Wilbur fell through the intact glass with a fading scream.

A distraught Royston rushed to the library door; he had seen all that he needed to. It was still locked.

"Help!" his father's voice screamed again.

Royston had no choice but to watch the replay of the death on a precise loop several times over.

"I know what you're trying to do!" he thought to himself, making certain she couldn't revel in his despair. Though he couldn't see her, he knew she was watching. Mocking him with her games. "You want to drive me mad enough to follow my father through that window, don't you?" he spoke in his mind. "The only way you want me to be able to leave this room is through the glass. Just like he did."

"Help!" his father shouted again.

"Will you shut up, you old fool?" he yelled at the spirit as he watched him back away to his death once more. This was not the way he had intended to say his goodbyes to his father and get his closure.

Royston began to launch some of the heftier hardbacks from one of the tall bookshelves at the panels of the door in order to splinter it, he even launched a couple at his father's spectre out of frustration.

Once the bookshelf had been emptied enough so he was able to move it, albeit with a struggle. He shuffled it to the window, obscuring much of the glass. There would be no way he would be falling through it now.

The continued loop of his father's last moments was broken. The door to the library flung open.

Royston spent no time wasted in his retreat from this infernal room.

The destination was a short one, only as far as the neighbouring study. He made a frantic grab for the vintage scotch, and then for another unopened bottle of liquor, just for good measure.

# 15

"I'll be back around half-eleven," Cliff Drakeford informed his son. "It's an away game down the Bells in Bluxley, so it's a minibus job back. It's a top-of-the-table match tonight. If we win, which I expect we will, there'll be a lot of beers consumed before shut tap, that's for sure. Beer always tastes sweeter when it's drank rubbing the salt into your rival's wounds; especially when it's on their own turf."

He let out a mischievous laugh, which suggested maybe he'd already made a start on the beers.

His gaze turned to Willard and Tommy.

"You boys help yourself to anything in the house that's age appropriate, and don't get into any mischief I can find out about. There's some money on the sideboard for a video rental. Again, make sure it's age appropriate. I don't want another Flesh Gordon incident."

The trio of boys laughed in unison as they recollected in their collective minds the time they had succeeded in tricking Cliff into picking up a copy of the softcore sex parody Flesh Gordon for them on VHS, having convinced him it was the family-friendly Flash Gordon with an innocuous typo.

Cliff too smiled as he recalled how much fun he'd had with that videotape once Drake had been scolded and sent to bed. The fact he'd rented it five separate times since then was his own little secret, which only he and the unjudgmental employee at the video store would know about.

Five minutes after Cliff had left for his night of throwing sharp objects whilst under the influence of alcohol, there was the sound of knocking at the front door, adding to the uneasiness growing within the living room of the Drakeford house.

Drake forced himself up from his chair to answer. As little enthusiasm as he held for going through his late mother's belongings, he had just as little for inviting Finch into his home.

Finch's greeting was little more than a grunt as he saw Drake open the door to him. As unenthusiastic as the neanderthal sound may have been, it was a gesture of warmth and energy in comparison to Drake, who didn't make any motion other than for his unwanted guest to follow him to join the others.

"Hey," Finch spoke to Willard as he threw him a wave of the hand. It was clear he was warming to him.

"Get a room," Tommy wanted to quip, but wisely chose not to. The school bully appeared perfectly indifferent to him, and that was how he wished things to stay.

"Okay," Willard conducted. We may as well not waste any time over this."

# 16

"That's a lot of boxes," Tommy spoke as he climbed the ladder resting against the landing wall and peered into the attic. Drake was already up there and had switched on the light. Fortunately, the loft had been fitted with electrics, which saved them the arduous task of looking through everything by torchlight. Willard and Finch came up from behind to join them.

The boxes were stacked in a pyramid formation against the side wall, mirroring the shape of the roof.

"The Gazette was in publication for a long time," Drake confirmed. "Mum sorted each box by years of issue. At least that will help us rule out some of the oldest crates. But still, one edition a week, fifty-two editions a year. Even if we narrow what we're looking for down to a ten-year period, that's still potentially over five-hundred papers we're searching through."

"So, my grandfather started the parties in October 1937. If Tommy and Drake focus on papers around those years to see if there's any incidents or scandals which caused them to stop, Finch and I will cover the years 1950 onwards."

Finch showed Tommy and Drake the photograph his father had left them and pointed to the presumed father and son at the end of the group.

"Also keep an eye out for these two. We need to know who they are, and if they're still alive."

"Just remember guys," Drake made a point to add. "Please leave this attic, and more importantly, those boxes, exactly how you found them. If my dad finds out we've been snooping through this stuff it will be me haunting you pricks as a vengeful spirit instead."

**********

An hour had passed.

The four boys had still to find what they were looking for amongst the reams of pages. Their progress had not been aided by the necessity to be so delicate and making sure everything was placed back exactly how it should have been; even Finch had been abiding by Drake's request.

Their increasing frustrations and disheartenment was suddenly lifted by an excitable squeal from Willard.

"Guys," he shouted.

The enthusiasm in which he called out suggested that this was his, 'Eureka,' moment.

Finch, who was the closest, was the first to lay eyes on the photo Willard had been pointing at. He recognised the faces in an instant. They were the two unidentified people in his father's photograph.

Their moment of victory was fleeting, however. Upon reading the accompanying headline, their spirits were sunk.

### Local Businessman and Son Die in Tragic Car Accident.

Though neither said it aloud, the look they gave each other spoke enough words. Their theory was right, everyone in that photograph, bar one, had met an untimely and unnatural demise, meaning Royston Jennings would be next, and they didn't believe he had much time.

"Wait!" Willard proclaimed. "The report says there was a survivor."

Finch quickly scanned the wording below the photograph.

Local businessman, Saul "Cherry" Bakewell, lost control of his vehicle going outward on the A38.

Both Saul Bakewell (48) and Gregory Bakewell (17) were pronounced dead by the emergency services at the time of arrival. Mr Bakewell's wife, Amanda Bakewell née Symmons, was found with serious injuries but is expected to survive.

The boys' focus was diverted by a sudden scream of fright. They instinctively turned and saw Drake, scuffling backwards by his hands and feet. His face was a picture of terror.

"Look out!" Tommy screamed at him as Drake retreated closer towards the open attic hatch.

Drake's body flipped backwards through the opening. His descent was abruptly halted as he felt something grab tight onto his left leg. The abrupt halt caused his body to slam hard against the ladder, yet it was a preferable injury to landing headfirst against the landing floor, and an almost certain broken neck.

"I got you, numbnuts," Finch grimaced as he struggled against the strain of holding the nine-stone teenager. His legs, in turn, were being supported by Tommy and Willard.

As Finch observed Drake's face, the look of fear and panic was engraved upon him. He was certain the fright wasn't caused by the shock of the fall.

"She's up there, she's up there!" he repeated. The tears were clear in his eyes.

"I'm going to have to let you go," Finch strained. "I can't hold on for much longer. I need you to straighten your arms out, to break the fall. It won't be much of a drop for you. You got that?"

More babbling was returned that Finch couldn't decipher, yet Drake extended his limbs as asked. At least it meant he was coherent enough to listen.

"Good lad. I'm going to let you go on the count of three, ok? Make sure your arms are strong and tense. One. Two. Three."

His drop was an awkward looking one, but no damage was done upon his ungraceful landing. Nonetheless, Finch was quick to follow him down via the far more conventional way of the ladder, to check upon him.

"We'll call that a down payment on the beating I owe you," Finch stated, before giving Drake a hefty jab to his arm, before smiling and patting him reassuringly on his shoulder." That's the rest of it. We're even now, right?"

The punch was enough to bring Drake's frightened mind back to his surroundings. Finch shepherded him away from the ladder to allow room on the landing for Tommy and Willard to join them.

"I saw her," Drake spoke again as he began to sob. His words were more concerted this time.

"The girl in a porcelain mask?" Willard probed. Drake shook his head in disavowal. Before composing himself to say the words.

"My mother."

# 17

Drake was sitting on the sofa with a mug of hot tea. His hands trembling as the image of his mother was still fresh, tormenting his mind. He feared it would remain stuck with him for the duration of his life.

His three companions were staring at him intently from their various positions in the living room. It was a look that told him they were desperate to hear more.

"I saw her," he complied. "Right by the box of her personal belongings. Her neck was twisted and loose, just as my dad had found her, after the accident." Drake paused for a moment and made an inadvertent touch of his neck as he contemplated a similar demise had almost been bestowed upon him. "She was standing there, staring at me, mouth open."

"Do you think she was trying to tell you something?" Tommy asked.

"I don't know. If she was, then she sure as shit has a messed-up way of doing so. She nearly killed me."

"Do you think we should go back up?" Tommy continued to press.

"No chance in hell," Drake was quick to dismiss. "We're done."

"Okay," Willard attempted to soothe. "I'll go back up and make sure everything is as it should be and get the ladder put away. You've been through enough already this evening."

*********

Willard had meticulously placed back the last few items which had remained left out before Drake's incident. He gave the place one more survey, to ensure nothing had been missed. He was more than satisfied with the results. Mr Drakeford would need a serious case of OCD if he were to suspect that anything had been moved, the next time he came up to the attic, whenever that would be.

Before he went back down to join his friends and closed the attic door, however, he knew he had one more thing to do, and would have to be quick about it. He didn't want to risk raising his friend's suspicions.

Just as Tommy had suggested, he too believed the spirit was trying to give Drake a message about something. Was it related to what they were looking for? Possibly. Was he going to take a look? Most definitely.

Drake said he had seen her by the box of his mother's personal belongings. Willard wasn't sure what he felt lousier over - the fact he was betraying his best friend's trust, or that he was about to go through his dead mother's most personal of possessions.

Willard displaced with delicateness various other trinkets and certificates, from what must have been her childhood. They revealed a leatherbound A5-sized Filofax with the words written in biro upon a white, sticky label fixed to the case.

### *Tragic accident, or something more at Hilltop Manor?*

The fastening to the Filofax was secured by a built in robust-looking six-digit combination lock.

The Filofax was small enough to be wrapped discretely within his sweater. He could use the strenuousness from moving the ladder back into the utility room as an excuse for wanting to take his jumper off in the cold October weather. He had never been more thankful for his scrawny frame to make this explanation seem plausible. He vowed he would return it to Drake as soon as able, with the hope his friend would be in a forgiving mood for him taking something so personal.

# 18

Willard didn't spend much longer at Drake's house following his return from the attic. He was eager to smuggle the contraband out of the house before there was any chance of detection.

Fortunately, for him, Drake wasn't as astute as Finch, who had asked him with misplaced pride what it was he had taken, as soon as they were outside the garden gate, and in the clear.

"I've shoplifted enough stuff in my time to know the old, wrap it in a jumper, trick," he teased.

The red flush upon Willard's cheeks was enough of a tell-tale sign to negate any proclamation of innocence he might have attempted.

"It's something belonging to Drake's mother," he spoke with shame. The act seemed even more lowly upon saying it out loud.

"Bloody hell. I've done some horrible shit in my time, but, that my friend, is next level. Remind me to install some CCTV cameras if you ever come over to my house."

"I think she was writing a report for the paper on what happened to the girl with the porcelain face," he spoke, hoping this would not only justify his actions to his companion, but stop him busting his balls a bit too. He showed off the Filofax.

Finch observed the handwriting upon the label with keen interest.

"I should be able to break the lock, there's bound to be some tools back home which that'll do the job."

"We're not going to do any damage to it," Willard defied. "It goes back to Drake exactly how we found it. Besides, it should be easy enough to work out the combination. It's only six digits, and stuff like that is often just a birth date."

"Well, I'll leave that with you to work on. It's been an eventful day, to say the least, and I'm spent. Besides, why do any more work when you have a lowly minion such as yourself who can fill you in on the important bits tomorrow?"

Finch slapped him playfully on the shoulder and said good night, leaving Willard by himself. It was only now the realisation befell him that he still hadn't been home since he made his abrupt exit in the morning.

The thought of heading back to Hilltop Manor didn't inject him with excitement. What if the girl with a porcelain face was to visit him again?

# 19

It was just past eleven o'clock by the time Willard returned to Hilltop Manor. His father was passed out, still clothed, downstairs on the living room sofa. The odour of liquor filled the air, and the empty bottle of scotch was knocked over beside the settee. Willard doubted the toppled bottle was the effects of any supernatural shenanigans though.

On this occasion, he decided not to be too judgemental about his father's excessive night of drinking. He had lost two of his best friends in the space of two days and was coming to terms with the inevitability he would be next, and soon at that.

Willard wished he could wake him, to tell him he was working on a way to stop that happening. To tell him everything would work out ok. To tell him, despite their differences, he loved him.

This wasn't the way this family of two did things, however. Instead, he would just place a blanket on him and leave some water and Alka-Seltzer on the nearing coffee table, for when he awoke.

He made his way up the flight of stairs and straight to his room. He threw down his backpack on the floor and gently placed the Filofax upon the bedside table before bellyflopping onto his mattress in a dramatic display of his tiredness. He let out a dejected sigh that suggested he wasn't done with what had already been a most arduous day just yet.

Willard rolled over onto his back and attempted a blind reach towards the top of the bedside table. It took a couple of efforts to place his hand back upon the Filofax. He pulled it toward his chest. At least the combination would be straightforward to crack, he thought to himself - perhaps too smugly.

His first attempt was Kimberley Drakeford's birthday. He had been to her grave a few times, accompanying Drake for support as he laid flowers on her stone. March 26th, 1949. The date had stuck with him since, and how young she had been taken from this world. Willard wasn't certain now that it had been an accident at all.

2-6-0-3-4-9

No success.

0-3-2-6-4-9

Nope.

Undeterred, he tried Drake's birthday. Thinking of it, that should have been his first guess anyway.

1-7-0-2-7-1.

Nothing.

0-2-1-7-7-1.

"For god's sake, why won't you open? You Filofax Fuck!"

Remembering Cliff Drakeford's birthday had been more of a challenge for him to recall.

He could recollect the month easily enough, it was May, and he could only recount that much because of the time Drake had told them on the way to school the morning after his father's fortieth birthday party how drunk his dad had been.

Willard always loved hearing stories from Drake about his beloved father, even though on occasion his enjoyment of the anecdotes had been tainted by hints of jealousy as he thought of what his father-son relationship was like in comparison. This particular story, however, Willard could remember as one he'd found more sad than humorous.

Mr Drakeford had come home from the social club after last orders, singing a godawful rendition of Dean Martin's Amore, using a traffic cone he had somehow acquired as a megaphone. He had then started a melancholic conversation with Drake's mother about how hard he was trying to keep his life together following her death and that he forgave her for the secrets he knew she was hiding from him.

Kimberley Drakeford had been dead for several years at this point. Yet, knowing what he knew now, Willard was starting to wonder if he really had been talking to her.

Willard spent the rest of his waking night, attempting every combination possible for Cliff Drakeford's birthday, but there was no success.

Maybe it was another family member's birthday or anniversary. Knowing those dates was far beyond his knowledge and something he wouldn't be able to gain without raising suspicion.

"Hey Drake, out of curiosity, when was your parent's anniversary?" or, "Hey Drake, I was wondering what date your late grandmother's birthday is."

Maybe, Kimberly Drakeford wasn't as sentimental as he had hoped she was after all. Maybe, the combination was a random pre-set one, straight out of the box.

He would have to keep working on combinations for as long as he could, before having to take Finch up on his offer of breaking the lock. Until then, perhaps they would have better luck finding Amanda Bakewell.

His father didn't have much time.

# OCTOBER 30, 1985

# 1

Even Mrs Weyland had to admit her cleaning services for Hilltop Manor, three times a week, were quite excessive. From her experience, an intensive clean from top to bottom, would only take her a day and a half at most.

Being an honest woman, she raised this point with Royston Jennings when he'd first hired her. Yet he dismissed her concerns and insisted, with assertion, she turn up for work three times a week anyway, and she would be paid well for those days.

She suspected he had employed her for the surplus day more for company than her deft hand with a duster.

Today was her second of her scheduled cleaning days of the week and, not wanting to take money for nothing, she had long ago perfected her routine to ensure she would be busied during these three days.

The first day her focus was on the upstairs and today she would concentrate on the downstairs. On her third visit of the week, she would give both floors a once over.

Mrs Weyland was surprised to see Willard by himself in the dining room upon her arrival. The sight of his father sat in the dining room, reading the morning paper, was as much as an inevitability as night follows day.

"Where's your father?" she asked with genuine concern.

"He's sleeping off a heavy night," the answer came. Willard gestured drinking from a bottle for good measure. Mrs Weyland appeared taken aback.

"I never had him down as much of a drinker."

"He's not," the blunt riposte came. "I think you're going have to clean around him today Mrs Weyland as I have a feeling he won't be moving far from the sofa."

"I'll be sure I won't use the hoover too much in that case, I'm not sure he'll appreciate the noise."

"Mrs Weyland, whilst you're here, can I ask you something please?"

"Of course, my dear. As long as it's not about the birds and the bees. I taught my son so well about those, the only thing that turns him on now are spotted tits covered in honey!"

Mrs Weyland let out a mischievous laugh at her own joke. Hearing her heartfelt guffaw was enough to bring a smile to Willard's distant demeanour.

"I'm sorry," she spoke once her amusement at herself had petered out and she remembered what had started it. "You wanted to ask me something, didn't you?"

Willard nodded.

"Do you remember any talk about the Halloween parties which used to happen here in my grandfather's time?"

Her jovial expression morphed to one more nervous upon this question. She let out a sigh and pulled up a chair.

"Are you sure you don't want to hear about the birds and the bees instead?" she attempted to laugh off.

Willard's gaze stood steadfast in defiance.

She repeated her heavy sigh for good measure. As much as she enjoyed her conversations with the boy, she was uncomfortable when it came to talking about his grandfather with him – she still hadn't forgotten how close she came to losing her job over mentioning his suicide all those years ago.

This particular question, however, brought with it a different level of awkwardness. Nonetheless, he wasn't a young child anymore, and, as such, she wouldn't treat him as one.

"I would have been in my late teens when they first took place, I never got to go to any though. They were exclusively for the miners and their families, to say thank you for their service. My parents never worked in the mine either, so as such, an invite always evaded our family."

"Do you know why they stopped?"

"There was some kind of nasty accident one of the years. Some poor girl died. I wouldn't be able to tell you her name though. Nor would I be able to tell you how it happened. Details from that night were very guarded, and no one who was there talked about it. I do know two things for sure, though. Firstly, they stopped the parties after that night. And second, it's bad luck to talk about it.

My parents, God bless their holes, were never superstitious or religious people. Not one little bit. But even they believed bad omens befell those who knew what happened. Real bad omens.

Usually, with scary stories, local myths, and urban legends of that ilk, they always find a way to be told. They survive, evolve, and live on through the ages, but not this one. That story died with my generation. I don't think anyone really knows what happened that night anymore, no one living anyhow - and it's probably for the best.

I'm not a religious or superstitious person either, I don't believe in that kind of claptrap, What I did believe in, however, was my parents, and if they were too scared to speculate aloud what could have happened, well, that tells me you'd be best served to forget about it too.

Why don't you think about normal things teenagers do instead? Like sniffing glue in the park or something."

"Thank you," Willard spoke. "Can I ask you something else? Something unrelated?"

He hated lying to Mrs Weyland, but with her knowledge of the townsfolk - those more cynical would say nosiness - asking her would be quicker than trawling through the Yellow Pages.

"Of course."

"Did you ever know an Amanda Bakewell?"

"Wow, that's a name I haven't heard for a long while. What's this about Will?"

"Oh, it's some homework assignment from school and she came up in an old Gazette, something about surviving a car crash."

"If you can even call it surviving. The accident took everything from her. Her family, and her mind. I'm not sure if it was the injuries from the crash, or the trauma, but let's just say her and reality haven't been bosom buddies ever since. It wouldn't be cruel of me to say she'd have been better off dying in the accident too.

From what I understand, she's spent the last five or six years at Blossom Tree Residential Home. If I ever end up in that place Will, do me a favour, watch One Flew Over the Cuckoo's Nest, so you know the best way to smother me with a pillow."

Willard pounced with speed from the kitchen chair and made a beeline for the doorway.

"Hey!" Mrs Weyland called out to him. "What's going on?"

"Don't worry," he shouted back. "I'm just off down the park to sniff some glue."

# 2

Wendy Farrow anticipated an uneventful morning behind the reception desk of Blossom Tree Care Home, as was often the case in her employment here.

She was hesitant to refer to it as a graveyard shift since this place was nothing more than a pitstop on the way to the grave for many of the residents here.

Yet, no matter what she elected to denote the morning shift as, there was no hiding from the fact nothing much of any note ever happened front-of-house during these hours.

It was certainly rare to receive any visitors before 11:00, and an even rarer occurrence for those visitors to be so young.

Upon hearing the irritant that was the buzzer, signifying the front door had opened, she peered, suspiciously, over the top of her paperback of Danielle Steel's Secrets – a book which was only serving as an unnecessary reminder of just how boring her job, let alone her life, really was.

She was greeted by the sight of four teenage boys. Despite their truancy, they were still dressed in their Bleddington Comprehensive school uniforms. With a collective purpose, they walked up to the reception desk and stared at her intensely, as if they were extras from the movie, Scanners.

"Er, can I help you?" she asked with trepidation, knowing it was a question she was going to regret.

"We're here to visit Amanda Bakewell," Willard spoke with far more confidence than he was feeling internally.

"I'm sorry dear," the receptionist's answer came. "It's family visits only, I'm afraid."

114

Undeterred, Finch sensed his opportunity to take the lead.

"But we're with the school program."

This unexpected and confident response was enough to throw some doubt into Wendy's mind.

"What school program?"

She had already taken the bait.

"It's a new initiative between the school and Blossom Tree. Volunteer pupils are assigned a resident here and we were given a Mrs Amanda Bakewell. You should have been sent a letter from Mr Grenfield."

"I don't have anything here to say you were coming."

"That's just typical of the British postal system," Finch sighed. "You'd have thought they'd have delivered it by hand, being local and all."

"It's okay, Johnny," Tommy intervened.

If they were lying about some fictitious school program, they may as well double down and lie about their names too.

"I have a copy of the letter from Mr Grenfield, in case of any issues."

The forged document wasn't professional enough to stand up under any scrutiny in a court of law, but the boys had all been in agreement it would at least be convincing enough to trick a poorly paid receptionist for a care home.

Finch had pilfered a stash of school letter-headed paper several months earlier upon one of his summonses to the headmaster's office for a stern lecture about his behaviour. It had been an acquisition which had saved him multiple beatings from his father. He had constructed many a false correspondence on this purloined stationary as cover for his truancy or faltering grades. For this particular letter, he had even gone all out this morning, and used his father's typewriter – he'd never even put that much effort into any of his legitimate schoolwork.

The receptionist examined the page and didn't question its authenticity.

"I mean, if you have any concerns, you can always call the school, or your manager." Finch pushed further, almost as if to challenge her.

Wendy smiled and handed the letter back. Calling the manager would entail having to endure a conversation with her, and that prospect was as enticing as bellyflopping onto a bed of cacti. Besides, she wanted to get back to her book.

"Okay, boys, she's in Room 11. Though I fear you've been lumbered with the short straw on this one. She's not, how should I say, the most coherent of residents, even at the best of times. You may find any conversations a bit on the erratic side. But even so, I'm sure she'll be glad of some fresh blood to talk to. Just don't take anything she says to heart. When I buzz you in, tell the on-duty orderly you're here to visit Amanda Bakewell, and he'll sort you out."

# 3

"I'm not sure I'm comfortable with all four of you going in to visit her," the orderly, Jim Grey, declared upon hearing a similar spiel as what Wendy had been given.

It was clear in an instant this employee wasn't going to be swayed as easily as the receptionist. If they dared chance or push their lie any further, they would risk blowing the whole charade.

The boys nodded with submissive obedience.

"She's easily enough agitated as it is," Jim continued. "And having a group of strangers, well-meaning or otherwise, will just run the risk of setting her off."

After a prolonged moment of internal deliberation, Jim Grey spoke again.

"I tell you what, I will let two of you in, so as not to overwhelm her. I'll be outside the door listening like a hawk for any commotion. If, at any moment, I think my resident is getting herself worked up, you're out of there in a heartbeat. You got it?"

They had no choice but to agree to his conditions.

"The other two, you're here as a school initiative to keep the resident's company, right? Well, I haven't been briefed on any such schemes, but I'm willing to take your word on that. I mean it's not something anyone would exactly lie about, is it? It would be messed up if they did. In any case, there's more than one resident here. There are plenty of lonely old souls that would have their day made for some company. I'll be sure to feed it back to your headmaster that you went above and beyond for your scheme. Hopefully, you'll even gain some extra recognition for it."

The boys' huddled together suspiciously in an audible which would have been more suited to the NFL than a peaceful nursing home. When they emerged, they informed the orderly it would be Willard and Finch who would go in to speak with Amanda Bakewell. Drake and Tommy would have to go to wherever Jim Grey would send them.

# 4

The look Amanda Bakewell's face displayed as she laid eyes upon the two teens was not the one Jim Grey expected when introducing them to her. A slight smile invaded her weathered face, their presence seemed to reassure her.

"You two look just like your grandfathers," she spoke with a friendly welcome.

The orderly shrugged off the comments from the resident as more delusions.

"Are you happy for these two young men to sit and keep you company for a while?" he sought to clarify with her in an almost patronising manner.

"Of course, Jeff. I've been expecting them for a long time now."

Jim threw the boys a look which suggested, "good luck, you're going to need it," and left the room.

Once the door was closed and the boys were alone with her, she burst out into an infectious cackle.

"I'm just teasing him, I know his name's not Jeff, I just like to mess. I know full well his name is Dave. You two really do look like your grandfathers though. Can't deny that. It's like staring at a couple of ghosts, and I've seen my fair share of those in my time. I'm guessing you have too. That's why you're here, visiting this crazy old bat, isn't it? You've seen, her?"

The teens nodded their confirmation in perfect symmetry.

"I'm truly sorry," she empathised. "If you've seen her, she's already got you marked for death.

Your bitter end most likely won't come for a long time yet. Maybe not even until you reach your father's ages.

Don't mistake that as a reprieve though. It's the cruellest of curses.

If a free man learns they don't have long to live, very often, that's when they finally start living. They see their life for what it is, a gift. They begin to appreciate every day on this earth could be their last and try to fit as much into it as they can, with what little time they have left.

There's always a flipside, however.

For someone on death row, unable to leave their prison, which for you boys, that's what Bleddington is, then waiting for their death to come is the cruellest of curses. Maybe that's why she waits so long to take you out. She lets the idea of your inevitable demise fester and rot inside of you. She kills a piece of you each day without you even knowing, until you're just a shell of the stranger you remember yourself once as.

Have you ever wondered why you and your fathers have never left Bleddington? If I had a vengeful spirit coming for me in a town as small as this, the first thing I would do is to hightail it and get far away from here, right? It's like that killer shark movie. If you don't go in the sea, it can't bite you. It's the easiest of solutions. In, her, case, however, she's not shackled by the same confines.

She wants you to play her twisted game by her rules. If you try to run from the water, so to speak, you will only end up deeper in quicksand instead.

If it's any consolation, at least you have someone who believes you, and that's the only real difference between crazy and sane, right? When Saul told me about her, I didn't believe a single word. I thought he was trying to scare me as a bit of playful teasing. I could see it in his face though. He believed it alright, and he believed it well enough.

My apologies boys, I'm rattling off at a hundred miles per hour and getting a bit ahead of myself, as I often have a want to do.

I was Saul's second wife, you see. His first, Dawn, hung herself before we met.

I moved to Bleddington, to work as a secretary for the tin mine, and I met Saul through your grandfather, Wilbur.

Our relationship was a whirlwind romance, as they call it, and we were married within the year.

Wilbur was best man at our wedding, you know. And your grandfather, Edwyn Finch, was the groomsman. I would say small world, but in a town this size, there's seldom ever any coincidences involved.

Once again, I digress.

November 17th, 1956, Saul woke my stepson, Gregory, and myself in a panic. It couldn't have been any later than half-six in the morning. This old, failing brain of mine may not work so well anymore, and I often struggle to distinguish real memories from the fabricated ones. Yet this one is as vivid as any.

He kept shouting, 'I've seen her, I've seen her. We have to leave Bleddington right now. It's our only chance. She isn't going to get us like she did the others.' I would have thought he was in the midst of a mental breakdown of some kind, but when hearing these words, Gregory was starting to panic too.

The best thing I could do was to play along and humour them both until they calmed down and returned to some form of reality.

I'd heard of collective hysteria before and, somewhat naively, put it down to that. I asked Saul, 'Where would we go? What about our house? What about our friends? What about Gregory's school? He was seventeen at the time.'

None of this practical stuff seemed to matter to either of them. They only knew they had to leave - immediately.

Saul kept repeating that we had to get as far away from this town as possible. He said we had more than enough money in the bank to buy another house somewhere. We even had plenty of savings to live out of hotels for as long as we needed to if it came down to it. All we had to do was drive and keep on driving.

You can't run from your fate though. All it does is speed it up.

I told Saul I'd drive. I mean, I had no choice but to. He was in no fit state to get behind a wheel, and Gregory hadn't got his licence yet, not that he was any calmer than his father."

The teens watched as the tears streamed down the cheeks of the old lady.

Conflicting emotions caught both of them off guard. They were desperate for her to finish the story, yet they didn't want to witness her under further duress.

Then there was the orderly to consider. He said he would be outside the door in case the resident became agitated, and though they doubted he would be able to listen to her muffled words from outside the room, should she break down, they were certain he'd hear her cries.

Amanda wiped her face with the sleeve of the care home-issued nightgown she was still dressed in. She had composed herself enough for now to continue.

"Saul was beside me in the passenger seat and Gregory was in the rear. We were ten miles or so from Bleddington, and on the A-Road to the M5.

Saul had calmed down a little, now that we had left the town, but he still said nothing. Gregory was quiet too. He had a look on his face I'd never seen before. Usually, he had a sweet and gentle demeanour about him, but that day he wore a debilitating look of guilt and regret.

My eyes had been focussed on the road when the hysterical screaming, coming from the back seat, filled the air. I couldn't see what it was that had set Gregory off, but he was freaking out and staring at something next to him. He was petrified, yelling aloud that he was sorry, over and over again.

Yet nothing was there. Nothing I could see anyway. Saul could see it though, and he made a panicked grab for the steering wheel. We veered onto the wrong side of the road. I couldn't wrestle the wheel back in time to avoid the oncoming truck.

I must have blacked out from the impact of the crash, but when I came to, Saul's body was next to me. A shard of glass from the broken windscreen had pierced his jugular. He had bled to death. Dear, sweet, Gregory, was dead in the back seat. His neck had been snapped from the force of the collision - or so the coronary report had said.

As my eyesight began to focus from within the wreckage, that was when I saw her. A girl with a porcelain face.

She was standing a few metres away, staring at me with a cruel intent.

I blackened out again. I can't tell you whether it was from the injuries or from fear. All I can tell you is that when I came back around, I was in the hospital."

The boys could see the resident's tone and body language was starting to become more animated as she stood to her feet.

Her calm, dignified demeanour, she had displayed until now, had vanished in an instant. She waved her arms wildly in the air with no meaningful coordination and her gaze looked distant. Her voice was getting louder and more agitated as her eloquent and gentle posture had been vanquished by feral aggression.

"That was nearly thirty years ago, but the pain is still now. The memories are an open wound, festering and spreading throughout me like an infection which can't be cured.

I still see them from time to time, Gregory, and Saul. I see them in my room, staring at me helplessly, yet I never know whether they're really there or if it's my broken mind playing tricks. I'm tired of living this way. I'm tired of having the only thoughts of any real clarity being those of the accident. I'm tired of seeing her taunting face as my family lay dead around me. But most of all, I'm just bloody tired.

I don't know why she spared me all those years ago, maybe the life she left me with was vengeance enough. Whatever her reason, I've suffered my penance and deserve to rest in peace and be with my family again. I'm done playing her games."

Her voice levels were nothing less than a shout now. Loud enough for Jim Grey to come rushing in to try and calm her. If he couldn't do it with words, the premade cocktail of medication primed inside the syringe he held in his hand would certainly bring her down.

"Precious Harper, you bitch, I'm ready for you. Get me, come on, what are you waiting for, you cunt?"

The steward made an impressive beeline toward the woman. If he registered the boy's presence, he paid them no acknowledgment. His focus was on Amanda and her alone. He drove the needle into the meat of her arm, like Van Helsing driving a stake through the heart of his adversary.

Willard and Finch used this as their opportunity to leave undetected whilst the steward's attention was still on the resident. It was one thing them being there under false pretence, it was another having to face further interrogation from the orderly once the situation had calmed.

"Tommy! Drake!" Willard yelled as they ran down the corridor. As soon as he called their names, he could sense the disapproving gaze of Finch upon the back of his neck. 'You fool,' he imagined his mentor's thoughts berating. 'Never use our real names.'

Willard was sure he even called out 'sorry,' behind him.

A few members of staff came into the halls to see what the commotion was about, Tommy and Drake with them.

The sight of their friends fleeing was all the indication they required to suggest they should follow suit.

The four boys sprinting past the reception desk was enough to draw Wendy's attention from the next page of her book. They had exited the building before she even had the chance to ask what the hell was going on.

"Well, that didn't go as we planned," Tommy wheezed as he attempted to catch his breath once they had run far enough from the residential home to be sure they hadn't been followed by any staff.

"I wouldn't say that" Willard wheezed. "We know the girl with a porcelain face's name now."

# 5

Willard and Finch spent little time wasted in heading to the cemetery of St Peter's church, upon hearing the true name of the girl with a porcelain face.

Drake had opted to return to school instead of playing Columbo with ghosts. It had not gone unnoticed by the group that he had become more introverted since seeing the spectre of his mother, and the thought of going to a graveyard, where there would be an abundance of potential spirits, was proving too much for him to process.

Despite Tommy thinking, justifiably so, this was the most exciting thing to have ever happened in his life, he didn't waste a moment in offering to return with Drake.

"Ghosts are something I didn't even think existed until yesterday," he proclaimed. "But best friends are something I've believed in every day."

"Dickhead," Drake quipped back, though not without a wavering tone present in his voice.

********

"Have you noticed anything strange about a lot of these gravestones?" Finch asked as Willard and he made their way through the rows of the cemetery.

Willard had to confess he hadn't. Not that he'd been looking for anything out of the ordinary. The only thing his focus had been on was finding the grave of Precious Harper.

"The newer graves!" Finch hinted with little subtlety but to the same blank response. "Bloody hell, Jennings. You're supposed to be the intelligent one out of this partnership. I'm merely meant to be the musclebound, albeit incredibly charming, sidekick. It's easy to spot which stones are the newer ones from the amount of weathering to them. They stand out like a sore thumb."

Willard looked around and realised where Finch's thought process was coming from. It hadn't been anything he'd considered before, but why should he? He was taken aback by the higher-than-expected number of the newer-looking graves.

Willard examined the dates upon these stones and couldn't help but observe that a worrying amount of the departed had done so far earlier than natural causes would suggest.

It had taken the boys a further five minutes to find the gravestone of Precious Harper - at least, they could only assume it was hers.

The name upon the stone had been defaced to become almost illegible. The obscurement had been done with what appeared to be a chisel, or an object sharp enough to indicate this wasn't just some random act of vandalism. The grave had also been defiled by some graffiti, which Willard also suspected hadn't been random.

Although the paint had been attempted to be scrubbed away, the remnants of cruel words such as devil, monster and bitch could still be made out.

Conversely, Willard was sure he could make out the word, friend, written upon the stone in black marker pen in a handwriting he was certain he had seen before.

Any doubts the grave belonged to Precious Harper, were quelled by the two graves flanking it on either side. They read Keira Harper and Jeffrey Harper.

The boys reasoned to each other these two stones must have belonged to her parents.

Keira Harper's stone read.

Keira Harper
03-06-1919 to 12-09-1957

Beloved Mother and Wife.

Jeffrey Harper's read.

Jeffrey 'Harpo' Harper
03-04-1917 to 06-09-1956

Devoted Husband and Father.

"They both died so young," Willard observed.

"Yeah, and I have a feeling it wasn't from natural causes."

The stone of what they believed to belong to Precious said little outside her redacted name, just the dates.

17-01-1941 to 31-10-1955.

"Jesus," Finch spoke, she was only fourteen."

"Same age as me," Willard added.

# 6

Amanda Bakewell was in her room at Blossom Tree Residential Home, tackling the puzzle page in the daily newspaper.

Never being one for cryptic talk or riddles, she jokingly wished a slow and miserable death to the infidel who had written these devilish clues. Instead, she had elected to approach the crossword from a different direction than it had been devised for. She would fill in her own choice of words to see if she was able to complete the grid.

On one occasion, when Jim the steward had been passive-aggressively lecturing her about not doing the crossword right, she had decided to use the puzzle to have a bit of fun at his expense.

"That's not how you do it, Amanda dear," he stated with disapproval.

"Okay smartie-pants," she countered. "Let's see if you can do any better. Can you answer this one? Seven across. Postman's sack."

Jim looked deep in thought as he struggled to think of what it could be.

"How many letters are in it?" he asked.

"Bloody hundreds of them," she cackled before waving her middle finger proudly at him.

He never lectured her about doing it her way again.

She was pondering on what five-letter word, the second letter E, with C being the fourth, to write, when she looked up from the page and towards the window for some inspiration.

It was there she saw them.

Two figures in the corner of the room. The face of the older figure appeared middle-aged and had a wide gash torn into the side of his throat. A crimson trail displayed a constant oozing from the wound which dissipated to nothing.

The younger figure was a teenage boy. His head drooped limply to its side. A bulge of bone stuck out beneath the flesh from the opposing side of the neck.

Amanda had seen these spirits numerous times before, and though they frightened her on the first few occasions she had seen them, she had since grown to welcome their visits. Whenever they came to her now, she felt assured by their presence and would even talk to them as if they were still alive.

"Oh, my handsome men!" she proclaimed with joy, wiping happy tears from below her eyes. "It's so good to see your faces."

The spirits of Saul and Gregory had smiles now. They attempted to speak but no words could be heard. The more Saul tried to talk, the faster the crimson mist flowed from his wound.

Gregory's words were illegible, a rasping croak of noise was all that escaped.

Suddenly, their looks of happiness turned to sorrow. Then fear. Then, they disappeared.

In their place, the sobbing of a girl reverberated through the room.

"You got my message," Amanda challenged.

The pensioner had only blinked, yet when her eyes reopened a millisecond later, the girl with a porcelain face was in the corner of the room.

The figure took an unnatural step forward. The sound of bone snapping caused Amanda to cringe.

The resident's thin and frail hand made a reach for the pully beside her bed to call for assistance from the orderly. Yet she hesitated from pulling it as more sounds of cracking bone invaded her ears.

She doubted an orderly would see and hear what she could, and she also doubted they would be able to do anything regardless. Besides, she wasn't sure she even wanted their help.

Death was what she had asked for, and death had answered her call.

At last, she would be able to rest. To be with her family once more.

She withdrew her hand from the pully and instead wrote something down upon the crossword puzzle.

Peace.

Amanda smiled, then looked up to face the figure.

"I'm ready now."

# 7

With the school day still officially in progress, Mrs Weyland busy downstairs cleaning, and his father still on the sofa sleeping off his hangover, Willard took the opportunity to sneak to his bedroom undetected, in a further attempt to decode the correct combination for his Filofax nemesis. He couldn't help but attempt the disparaging calculation of how many combinations were possible for six digits. The contemptuous result was over sixty thousand, and he had so far attempted a little over a hundred of them.

With each failed effort, his edict that he crack the lock without breaking it, along with his relationship with his best friend as a consequence, was looking flimsier by the minute. Willard berated himself in his mind.

Afternoon was transcending into early evening, and his thoughts kept returning to the gravestone of Precious Harper. There was something he was neglecting; he was sure of it.

He pictured the image of the grave in his mind once more. Then it came to him. Perhaps the answer he had been searching for had already presented itself to him. Maybe, it was a birthday Mrs Drakeford had used for the combination after all. Precious Harper's birthday.

With no lost sense of smug satisfaction, Willard entered her date of birth from the stone.

1-7-0-1-4-1.

The result was the same as his previous failed efforts. The lock remained fastened.

Willard tried the different variations of the numbers,

0-1-1-7-4-1

4-1-1-7-0-1

4-1-0-1-1-7

Each bore the same infuriating outcome. It was all he could do not to smash the lock there and then, to hell with his best friend's feelings. But no, he would persevere for the rest of the day, he thought to himself - even if it would be the death of him.

Those words stuck in his head. The death of him. Maybe, it shouldn't be her date of birth he should be focussing on, but the date of her passing.

Willard moved the digits to, 3-1-1-0-5-5. The lock unfastened with ease – he was in.

# 8

The Filofax was open.

Willard's eyes were immediately drawn to the payment stub from a cheque, bound to the front page of an A5 notepad by a paperclip. He carefully removed the stub and spotted from the handwriting upon it, the amount was for twenty-thousand-pounds.

There was no mention of who the payment was from, but it didn't matter, he recognised the penmanship in an instant. It was his father's.

The handwriting on the notepad matched the front of the Filofax. The words were neatly written,

*The Death of Precious Harper - Accident or More?*
*An investigation by Kimberly Drakeford*

Willard removed the pad from the leather sleeve and two loose paper items fell from within the pages. He placed the pad on his bed and picked up the fallen debris from the floor.

The first item looked like it was an old photograph, the other was a handwritten letter from Kimberly.

The photograph had landed face down on the carpet. On the rear side in a handwriting he didn't recognise, he could see the words,

*Precious, 31st October 1955*

Was this a photo taken of her from the day she died?

A sense of nervousness came over him as he made a reach for the photograph. He would finally look upon the true face of the spirit.

As he picked the photo up and flipped it over in his hand, his nervous anticipation soon turned to sadness. The girl in the photograph, who he had to assume was Precious, was afflicted with Down Syndrome.

Although the photograph was black and white, he recognised the coat as the same red winter one she wore in her visits to him, along with the same yellow wellington boots.

He couldn't help but ponder how happy she looked. This in turn made him angry. Angry at how her life had been cut so short, and angry at his father for whatever role he had in her death.

Willard turned his attention to Kimberly Drakeford's letter.

My dearest Cliff,

Today I did something I swore I would never do. I betrayed my integrity for a payoff.

Even though the Gazette is a small-time paper for a small-time town, I still felt committed to telling the truth with my words, as I am doing to you now.

With Dominic so young, money so tight, and with us falling behind with so many payments, I had no hesitation in accepting a bribe for my silence. I did it to ensure we continued to keep a roof over our heads.

I am so deeply sorry I lied to you about the money coming from an inheritance from an estranged relative. Though I suspect you never truly believed that to be the case.

My investigation into the death of Precious Harper all those years ago has brought up a recurring theme of supernatural beliefs and curses.

Even though I do not believe in such things, I am
writing this letter as an insurance policy so the truth can
one day find a way of coming out, should anything
unforeseen happen to me.

Maybe, though, I'm just writing it to alleviate the
burden of my conscience that has been troubling me so. It
has been my one big regret in life.

Love,
Kimberly.

Willard placed the letter and photograph back with the
Filofax and proceeded to read the notebook. He could see
from the various scribbles and rewrites this piece was still a
work in progress and had never reached its conclusion
before his father had bought her silence.

# 9

The Death of Precious Harper - Accident or More?
An investigation by Kimberly Drakeford.

From 1937 To 1955, the annual Halloween party at Hilltop Manor had been a joyous affair.

For those who were invited, many looked forward to the occasion.

It was a tradition started by Wilbur Jennings as a way of combining his birthday with means of saying thank you to his workers of the Bleddington tin mine, numerous of whom risked both life and limb daily in his employment.

Even during the years of the second great war, when many of the miners had been called into service to their country, the festivities continued - though one can only speculate the atmosphere of those parties would have been a suitably sombre affair in their notable absence.

In 1955, however, the year of Wilbur's 50th birthday, a tragic accident happened that put an end to the Hilltop Manor revelries for good.

That day, October 31st, the reliably volatile Bleddington weather was astoundingly true to its unpredictable form, and a hellacious storm raged. Although the weather had calmed by the night, only the most resolute of partygoers felt confident enough in the elements to attend. Amongst them, a girl named Precious Harper, aged just fourteen.

Accounts from family, friends and neighbours say despite her challenges in life, due to her being born Down Syndromed, Precious had always set her heart and mind on one day attending the Hilltop Manor parties.

She often liked to pretend Hilltop Manor was a castle, and she would one day be a princess at a grand ball there.

Though life was no fairy tale for her, she believed this daydream to be her very own happy ever after.

Alas, since neither parent of hers worked for Wilbur Jennings, no invite was ever forthcoming. She did, however, have a fairy godmother, in her kindly neighbour, Katherine Dawset.

Knowing of Precious's yearning to go to the party, coupled with the fact her husband had started working the mine earlier that year, she had talked her son, Lance, into taking Precious in his parent's place. Sadly, he would turn out to be no Prince Charming.

Begrudgingly, the Harper's agreed to letting their daughter attend with Lance under two simple conditions. The first being she wore a mask so as not to bring any unwanted attention to her differences. A task they saw as not unreasonable since it was a Halloween party, and everyone would be costumed. The second condition, one more reasonable, was she would not leave Lance's side at all.

As judicious as these requests were, however, they were still ones the teenage boy would not abide by.

Boys will be boys, and even more so, teenage boys will be, well…. horny.

En route to Hilltop Manor, Lance had crossed paths with fellow teenager and perpetual classroom crush, Katie Groves.

Lance had been smitten with Katie for several years and found the idea of spending an evening in her company far more appealing than babysitting at a party for his father's rich employer.

When telling Precious their plans had changed for the evening, and they would not be attending Hilltop Manor after all, he was met with a more-than-justified tantrum from his companion.

Concerned her reaction, and her very presence, was making him look bad in front of his crush, he struck an ill-conceived deal with Precious. He would allow her to go to the party alone, whilst he went off with Katie. He would pick her up, at eleven o'clock, to take her home and, if their parents asked, they had been together all night.

What could ever go wrong?

The simple but tragic answer was everything.

Upon her ascent up the steep and rain-sodden steps to Hilltop Manor, young Precious lost her footing. She fell down them, and to her death, where her broken body was found by a couple of townsfolk running late to the party.

The events leading up to her death have never been disputed and have been verified by a number of statements. What can be disputed, however, is whether Precious's fall really had been an innocent accident.

Upon investigating this story and interviewing some of the surviving attendees (I shall be telling you more on that subject shortly) one of the gentlemen, who may have been more forthcoming about certain details than usual, due to indulging himself in a bit more alcohol than was appropriate for the hour of our meeting place at the Lamp and Canary inn.

Something he said about that night resonated with me far more than it should have. 'That damn Jennings' boy and his three imbecile rich friends. Those little brats almost made me jump out of my skin when I got up that damn hill.'

As soon as he had said these words, I observed his demeanour had changed. It was as though he realised he had already said too much. At first, he was hesitant - fearful almost - to say more, but after a few more drinks, of which I am ashamed to say I encouraged and paid for, he began to elaborate upon his comments.

Wilbur's son Royston (aged eighteen at the time) and three of his friends were fully embracing the Halloween spirit that year (and more than likely, some spirits of the other kind too) by hiding amongst the forage near the entrance to the house and jumping out and startling guests with their gruesome masks.

My intoxicated interviewee even informed me that he fell on his backside from fright when the boys jumped out at him.

Could it be he wasn't the only one who fell?

The distance between the steps and the entrance to the Hilltop Manor can't be more than ten meters. What if a young girl, alone, whose mind was not as old as her body turned to run and lost her footing on the slippery steps? Was her accidental death not solely down to the elements after all?

Upon gaining the identities of those in attendance, I was about to find out if what was, at first, intended to be a retrospective on the Hilltop Manor Halloween Parties would instead lead me to uncover a more nefarious affair.

Despite the extensive list of names which had been provided, it soon became clear that getting most of them to talk to me would be an exercise in futility. Not because they wouldn't be willing to, but simply because they couldn't. A concerning number of names on that list had since passed on.

What was more intriguing, albeit morbidly so, was that many of them had passed on relatively young.

What was more astounding about these deaths, again, albeit morbidly so, was many of them could not be attributed to natural causes.

The tragic mining accident of 1959 accounted for a substantial percentage of these fatalities - a disaster which sent shockwaves throughout the town. Yet a subtle ripple of further accidents seemed to hit the key players surrounding the accident.

Lance Dawset and Katie Groves, now an item, succumbed to a house fire during a party. Precious's parents were both killed in separate cases of apparent self-inflicted trauma.

For the parents of the four teenage boys who may, or may not, have been at the scene of Precious Harper's accident, they failed to fare any better.

Edwin Finch was victim to an unexplained and unsolved arson attack at his convenience store. Saul Bakewell, along with his son, perished in a car accident, and as for Franklyn Fisher, the local undertaker, if you haven't heard the stories yet, well, that's a tale nightmares are made of.

The fourth name of the teenage boy's parents stood out more than the others though. Wilbur Jennings.

Was it just a macabre coincidence so many of the guests that night met a premature end? My anonymous source didn't think so.

"We were given a workplace incentive, a fancy way of saying we were paid off, to agree with Wilbur Jennings' statement, and to never mention the accident to anyone." My source confirmed. "It wasn't that hard of a task to do in all actualness, since the investigating police officer, Pete Harker, was already in Jennings' pocket. Our statements were scripted for us, all we had to do was agree with that's what happened and sign them off.

In our defence, for what little it's worth, for all we knew, that was what did happen. After all, none of us actually did see that poor girl's death. What we did know for a fact, however, was no one dared to speak up. At first, because we all knew Wilbur Jennings had the means, and the money, to ruin our lives, but pretty soon it became apparent something else had the power to end it.

One by one, as we talked amongst ourselves about things that shouldn't be, it became apparent, as our numbers grew fewer, we had made a deal with the devil that would send us all to an early grave.

Some of those in attendance talked. Of course, they did. It was inevitable amongst a gathering of that size word would leak out. Yet their statements went unheard. No, that's not the right phrase to use. Their words were heard well enough, they just went ignored is all.

It would appear Jennings' coin was not without its limitations.

We began to hear talk with more and more frequency from our miner brethren sightings of a girl with a porcelain face. Those who mentioned seeing her would soon meet their untimely ends. Seeing her face was to see the face of death.

It became clear, to those of us remaining that is, the best way to prolong our already fleeting time upon this earth was to not mention her at all.

Even after Wilbur Jennings' so-called suicide, his son, Royston, who had now become our boss, kept the hush money coming, not that it was needed anymore. No one dared say anything. The fact I've even told you this story fills me with guilt. Not over what I've never said before, but guilt over me saying too much now. The more you know, the more you are likely to incur her wrath. I fear I have damned you too."

Willard noticed a teardrop had fallen onto the page from his face. The tears may have been his, but the sound of sobbing which began to fill the room was not. He looked up, to see in the corner of the room, Precious Harper. Willard no longer felt fear at the spirit, but an overwhelming sense of sorrow.

"I'm sorry for what happened to you," Willard sobbed, drying the tears with his sleeve. "Accident or not, they should never have covered it up."

The figure raised her arm.

The sound of her breaking bone when she moved had always caused him to wince, yet now as she elevated her decimated arm, he couldn't help but picture her tumbling backwards down the steps, each impact as she rolled, causing her bones to crack and displace further.

His eyes followed to where her twisted arm was pointing. She was pointing yet again to the old copy of the Gazette upon the bedside table.

Then, she vanished.

There was something about that paper that she was still trying to tell him, he was sure of it. But whatever it was, he couldn't figure out. He had read it thoroughly from front to back several times over since Mr Kready had given it to him in the classroom and, aside from the mention of his grandfather's party, he was certain there was nothing else in there relating to Precious Harper.

After painfully replaying the events of the past few days, since he had first seen the girl with the porcelain face, something Amanda Bakewell had said to him stuck in his mind.

"In a town this size, there's seldom ever any coincidences involved."

Willard bolted from sitting on his bed and made his way to the bookcase in the corner of the room, the corner from where Precious had just appeared to him.

# 10

Of all the people Mr Kready expected to open his front door to that evening, Willard Jennings was not one of them. One of the benefits which came with being regarded as the school bogeyman was that pupils left him well alone when outside the classroom.

"Jennings!" he proclaimed wearily after answering the knocking. "What are you doing here?"

"I've come to hand my homework assignment in, sir."

Mr Kready let loose with a thinly veiled sigh of disapproval. He didn't have much fondness for the boy during school time, but now he was standing on his doorstep, just after 17:00, his dislike of him had reached a new plateau.

"One of your friends has put you up to this for a dare, did they?" he questioned unimpressed. "At least it's different from throwing eggs at my window. Good evening to you, Jennings."

Mr Kready went to close the door but was thwarted by Willard's blocking of it with his foot.

"You really are pushing it, boy." The teacher's tone was full of ire.

"But I haven't given you my homework assignment yet," his defiance came as he pushed his hand through the gap of the ajar door, Kimberley Drakeford's notepad was clenched in it.

The door slowly opened fully wide.

"You better come in, Jennings," Mr Kready spoke, his voice not so harsh now.

*********

Willard couldn't help but survey Mr Kready's living room

out of nosiness from the settee he was sitting on. Finding himself in the home of the most-feared teacher in Bleddington Comprehensive was as momentous as Indiana Jones discovering the Temple of Doom.

For someone as strict and authoritative as his teacher, he expected the room to be well maintained, or at the least, tidier, but the room was scruffy and disorganised. Willard couldn't help but think it could do with a visit from Mrs Weyland for a day.

"I would offer you a soft drink," Mr Kready spoke. "But all I've got here is tea, water, or beer, and there's no way in hell I'm giving you one of my beers. Not because it would be irresponsible or you're underage, but because of the fact, they're my beers," Mr Kready propounded in an agitated tone which betrayed the hospitality he was trying to offer.

"I'm fine for a drink, thank you," Willard's reply came.

"So, that's what Kimberly Drakeford's final article was about." Mr Kready spoke as he held the notepad in his hand. He had yet to open it. "She told me she was working on something, a short while before she passed. She wouldn't tell me what though, just something that she knew I'd appreciate. When I'd asked her how things were coming along, the last time I ever saw her, she informed me she'd hit a dead end and had to knock the story on the head. There was something about her demeanour though that suggested to me she was lying."

"It wasn't just luck that I ended up having the paper with the story of my grandfather's parties, was it?"

"No, it wasn't. I'd set the pile of papers up so that when you came over in desk order, you'd specifically end up with that one. Nor do I think it was luck I ended up with that paper either.

I had asked Mr Drakeford for any surplus copies of the Gazette he was able to lend for my English class as I knew he had some old spares lying around the house, and I'd never thought to keep any of my old copies from when I was younger."

This statement surprised Willard somewhat. From the pile of weeks-old Telegraphs scattered about the place, he'd categorised Mr Kready as a bit of a hoarder.

The teacher continued.

"When I came to collect the papers from Mr Drakeford, he'd placed them all in a box in the hallway for me. We had a catch-up for old times' sake for about an hour before I left, and when I went back to the hallway, a loose newspaper was on top of the box.

At the time, I didn't think anything more of it. I just assumed it was another copy Cliff had found and put it on there when I was in the bathroom. When I got home and flicked through it, and saw the story about your grandfather's parties, it brought back the memories of Precious."

"She was your friend, wasn't she? I recognised the handwriting in marker pen on the gravestone. But to be sure, I checked through my exercise books from your English. The handwriting matched your markings."

"She lived across the road from here. If you take a look outside the window, her house was the one with the red door.

I was a few years older than her and used to babysit her on many an occasion. I was truly heartbroken when I found out about her accident. There was something about the events of her death which always seemed off to me. Your family were hiding something, I was sure of it, and I will always resent them for it.

I try my hardest not to let those feelings seep towards you, but whenever I see you, I can't help but see your family's faces. For that, I can only apologise. It is my flaw, not yours.

After seeing the newspaper, I thought I'd pay Precious's

grave a visit. It devastated me to see those things written on it. How people thought she was some kind of monster. Precious may have had her challenges growing up to the age she did, but she was the sweetest child and had the most infectious smile anyone could ever wish to see.

This may sound crazy to you, then again, maybe it won't, but the night of my visit to her grave, she came to me. Not, the Precious I remember but a broken figure with a porcelain mask for a face. I've heard the urban legends spoken about town that if you see her you die, well I'm still here, aren't I? She wasn't there for some murderous revenge; she was there as an old friend asking for help.

When she came to me, she was pointing to the copy of the Gazette and to the page with your grandfather's story in it. I didn't know what she was trying to tell me exactly, but I had the sense it had to do with her death.

That's when I figured I'd make sure you had it. You've always been an intuitive person and you would have the benefit of looking at it in a way I couldn't. You would look at it through the innocent eyes of youth, like Precious. Not some jaded middle-aged man like myself.

So, the big question now is, what happens next?"

# 11

Royston forced himself from the sofa.

He had slept through the best part of the day, and the diminished October daylight suggested to him the hour was now early evening.

The nausea he was greeted with upon his awakening made him regret in an instant his plan to drink his way through whatever punishment the girl with a porcelain face had in store for him. Not only was he still to incur her vengeance, but he was also to do so accompanied by the mother of all hangovers.

He doubted now that his demise would come to him tonight. She wouldn't be so merciful as to let him off from the suffering he had caused for himself.

Although he didn't have much of an idea of how he wanted to spend the remnants of his short time left in this life, he was certain he didn't want it to be stuck on the settee.

Whatever he would decide though, his only priority at this precise moment, was to make it to the bathroom before vomiting everywhere during his quest to find the holy grail of a toilet bowl.

After he had ejected everything from his body that he had been able to, and from whichever holes biology would permit, he had the far more enjoyable task of refreshing himself with a shower. Once clean and looking less like a cast member of the Evil Dead movie, he decided to make his way to the dining room.

He hadn't even read the day's newspaper yet, and though he knew it would have been presumptuous of him to expect it, he suspected the salt of the earth that was Mrs Weyland would have retrieved it from the letterbox upon learning of his incapacitation and left it on the dining room table for him.

Royston was destined to never make it as far as the

dining room, however. During his walk down the East
Wing, his eyes were drawn to the only other room in
Hilltop Manor than the upstairs library which remained
constantly locked.

The light seeped through from under the door of the
sitting room.

Such was the intensity of the beam; it was clear to
Royston that the light was being projected from a bulb
rather than what scant daylight remained during this hour
of the Autumn day.

He could hear a sweet, gentle, albeit muffled, singing
from within. He recognised both the singer and the lullaby
immediately.

Please hush, don't keep on crying,
My child with a lovely face.
**If you cry, you won't look as beautiful.**
And your mama's heart will be dying.

It was the song Constance used to sing to Willard before
he was born.

Despite his better judgement, like a sailor hearing the
siren's song, he was unable to resist the sweet voice. He
reached out to the doorknob and gave it a gentle twist. It
opened without any resistance.

He was greeted by the sight of Constance sitting in her
favourite chair within the room. The seat was angled
towards the large bay window overlooking the town.
Unlike Royston who found the view of Bleddington, and
the mine, less than visually appeasing, she had always
received great comfort in it. **Maybe, because she had been
the daughter of a miner and never forgot her modest
roots. It was through his Grandfather's Halloween parties
they had become introduced, then subsequently besotted
with each other.**

Beside the chair was a small table with a tray placed on
top of it. On the tray was her sewing box surrounded by

the scattering with the debris of fabrics and cotton wool. Despite the riches of her husband, and the knowledge she could have the finest teddy bears ordered from the most desirable embroiderers from London, she had been adamant that she make their child's first teddy bear from her own hands.

"The love in which I make this toy," she had told her husband, "will forever make it finer, more exquisite and more cherished than any purchased with the coldness of coin."

"Constance!" Royston spoke aghast. He knew she was a spectre, a vision. Yet to see her again, to hear her sweet voice, even to listen to that godawful lullaby again filled him with a joy he hadn't experienced in this house for far too long.

She turned. The singing stopped as she greeted him with the smile which had caused him to fall in love with her the first time he witnessed it and was enough to make him fall in love with her all over again every time she disarmed him with it.

"I can feel him kicking," she gushed as she placed her hand upon the swell of her pregnant belly. "I can't wait to meet our child," she further enthused.

With her free hand, Constance made a clasp for the small pair of scissors upon the tray beside her.

"Stop!" Royston yelled, but he was too late, she had driven the tip of the fabric scissors into the soft tissue of her stomach.

It was a motion she would repeat with fury several times over. Her white summer dress was now a scarlet robe as the blood seeped through with sickening speed. Constance cut through her flesh as if it were no different to the felt of the teddy she had been working on.

She began to sing her lullaby again, only this time, the sweetness of her melody was replaced by a spiteful tone he'd seldom heard from her mouth.

"Oh, my dear sweet beloved child,
Even though you'll be from my womb.
I promise I will never let you go.
From your cradle to my tomb."

Royston crumbled to his knees; all strength had gone from
him as he witnessed through tear-filled eyes as Constance
submerged her arm into the bloody open wound, she had
manufactured for herself.

As she withdrew, the foetus was in her clench.

"Isn't he beautiful?" Constance spoke with
wonderment as she gazed lovingly at the child.

She held him proudly aloft for Royston to inspect,
ignoring the river of blood flowing from her wound.

The new-born was twisted and broken, and its face was
not of human skin. It bore embedded into it, a cracked
porcelain mask.

Royston passed out. He had discovered what
Constance had seen in the void of the sockets of the girl
with a porcelain face in her final moments of life. This
vision was too much for him to bare.

When he came around, the room was as empty as it
had been for the last fourteen years.

# 12

Even under the limited view the lamp posts offered, Willard couldn't help but note the haunted look upon Drake's face as he approached him in Lenchley park. He imagined the look his friend displayed mirrored the one he had worn the morning after seeing Precious Harper for the first time.

The difference between them, however, was whilst Precious had been a complete stranger to him, the ghost Drake had seen in his attic had been the centre of his little universe for the first five years of his life.

When Willard phoned Drake from Mr Kready's house, he had told him he'd something of great importance to tell him and he needed to meet him alone. It was such an intriguing enticement; it would be impossible for him not to show up for the big reveal.

What he didn't tell him on the phone was that he had his mother's Filofax to bring him. If he had said that, he feared, justifiably so, their rendezvous would set off on a different footing to what Willard had hoped.

Drake had been sat on the swing, dragging the heels of his shoes against the soft surface of the ground. Upon seeing his best friend approach him he let loose with an almighty swing and dismounted at the pendulum's summit to show off.

It wasn't as impressive in execution as it had been in his mind, but at least he didn't fall flat on his face, or have the swing hit him in the ass on its return journey.

"That's got to be a perfect ten, right?" Drake spoke with optimism.

"Only if Stevie Wonder was judging," the quip was returned.

"So, how's my favourite Ghostbuster doing?" Drake jested, trying to put his own experience of ghosts to the back of his mind. "You've found a way to stop the girl with a porcelain face, haven't you?"

"I think so," the confirmation came. "But I need your help to do it. I think it will put your mum's soul to rest too."

Willard spotted an instant change in his friend's demeanour.

"What's this got to do with my mother?" his defensive snap came.

"By making right the one big regret my father took away from her."

Drake could only look at his friend with confusion. Whatever he was talking about, Drake wasn't privy to it, nor did he appear to like it.

Willard took a deep breath and took the Filofax from his backpack and handed it over.

"What's this?" he asked.

"Your mother's last article for the Gazette, she never got to publish it."

"And how have you got this?"

"I took it from the attic yesterday after you saw her. I think she was trying to show you where it was."

Drake swung a punch with his free hand into the jaw of Willard, sending him reeling to the ground.

"I deserve that," Willard stated whilst making a feel for his jaw.

"Yeah, you do," Drake confirmed as he pulled him back to his feet. "You've got to stop hanging around with murderous ghosts, they've turned you into a bit of an asshole."

The two of them stood in silence as Drake began to read through his mother's report.

"No wonder the girl with a porcelain face wants to rip your father's flesh off his face and take a steaming ghost shit into his eye sockets," Drake spoke wryly as an attempt to show there were no lingering hard feelings from him.

"I think she just wants the truth to be told. No more cover ups, no more pay offs."

"What about your father? we're talking manslaughter here. Are you willing to send him to jail?"

"I'd rather see him sent to a prison than a grave. Besides, if we do nothing, we're just continuing the cycle. We'd be just as damned as everyone else involved."

"So how are we going to do this, do we take this to the police or something?"

"We don't know if the police won't be paid off just like…" Willard almost said, "just like your mother was," but corrected himself before he risked unleashing the power of Drake's right hook once more. "Just like the others were," he concluded. "We need to get the story out there for the whole town to see, just as your mother's article was intended."

"Holy shit!" Drake declared as his mind caught up to Willard's intentions.

## 13

The hour was past 23:00 by the time Willard had returned to Hilltop Manor. It was only the adrenaline that was keeping him awake after yet another long day that had inflicted an unhealthy variety of emotions upon him. As he walked through the hall a part of him wondered if his efforts had been too late and Precious Harper had already enacted her revenge upon his father.

The boy was guided by a trail of turned-on ceiling lights along the east wing, leading to the sitting room. A sense of dread came over Willard as he approached it and saw the door ajar. It would be the cruellest of ironies that the room he had been born was also the same room he had lost both his parents in. Yet, as he approached closer, he could hear the sound of sobbing. This whimpering didn't belong to the girl with a porcelain face, it was his father.

Willard entered the room and saw his father sat on the chair angled towards the bay window. The room had a comfortable warmth to it where his father had ignited the coal within the fireplace. Even after all these years, it burnt without fuss. The smell of the fireplace was a satisfying one and disguised the stale smell of the room. As Willard approached the bay window, he could see the various house and street lights of Bleddington below, he noted that it looked far prettier in the dark than it did in the day.

Royston's whimpering stopped and he dried his eyes with the sleeve of his shirt.

"You're back late," he stated. "Been up to anything interesting?"

Willard was taken aback. This was the first time in far too long he could remember his father instigating a conversation with him. It was a shame he was about to railroad his efforts with questions of his own.

Willard threw something to his father which he instinctively caught. It was the leatherbound Filofax. One he had seen before. It would seem the girl with a porcelain face wasn't the only thing from his past that had come back to haunt him.

"I think we need to have that father-son talk that's evaded us for all these years," Willard spoke with assertiveness.

Royston emitted a heavy sigh.

"How much do you know?" he asked.

"Enough to know you had a hand in the death of a poor little girl and if she doesn't get her justice, you won't be long for this world."

Royston elicited a defeated smile and gestured for the boy to take a seat on the leather chair opposite the sofa.

"It seems like you already know enough."

"Not enough to fill in the blanks," he replied. "It was an accident. If you'd just told the truth about what happened instead of covering it all up, things could have been different. So many people could still have been alive, grandad, mother, your friends."

"Are you sure you want to do this Willard?" he spoke in a grave tone. "If you do, there's no turning back for you. Do you understand?"

"I think it's too late for that, father, it's fair to say there's already no turning back for me. And you've known that for all my life."

Royston's heavy sigh repeated before he drew a deep breath.

"It wasn't an accident," he declared.

"I don't understand."

"I mean, it was an accident in the fact we didn't mean for her to fall down the steps; of course, we didn't. That was just dumb tomfoolery on our part. It was meant to be a bit of Halloween hijinks, that was all. We didn't think she'd startle so badly though.

When Hux, Cherry, Sol and I jumped out at her from the hedges in front of the house, wearing our stupid Halloween masks, we really frightened her. More so than the others we'd pulled the same shit on. She turned to run, thinking we were real monsters, but the ground was so slippery following the storm earlier that day. She lost her footing and fell down the steps.

We chased after her as best we could, to try and stop her descent, but she tumbled faster than we could run. By the time we reached her, she was already at the foot of the hill, where her broken body lay.

She was still alive, barely, but her body was a mess. I sent the others up to get our fathers. They would know what to do. How to fix things.

As I stood over her, waiting for them, all I could hear were her cries of pain. It was the most godawful sound I've ever heard to this day.

I removed her porcelain mask, to see if I knew who she was. I didn't' recognise her, but I could see she was... different. She was also frightened, confused, and in excruciating agony. Even if she survived her injuries, she would have been severely crippled. As challenging as life would have already been for her, it would have been the cruellest of existences should she have lived.

Part of me tried to justify what I did next as a mercy killing. If she were a wounded animal, there would have been no hesitation in putting her down, it was the humane thing to do. But that wasn't the reason, and she knew it. The truth was, I was scared, I was confused, and I just wanted that damn crying to stop.

I grabbed her throat and started to choke the life out of her. She instinctively struggled against it as best as her broken body would allow, but it wasn't enough. She was soon dead at my hands.

My father and the others, they all saw it happen as they made their way down the steps. They didn't try to stop me though. They already knew it would be more convenient to explain a dead body which had fallen down some slippery steps than it would a crippled one who could tell of what had caused her accident.

Our fathers convinced us to leave her body there and wait for somebody to find it. In the meantime, we'd all go back to the party as if nothing happened.

About half an hour later, she was discovered by some latecomers. Word inevitably got to the rest of the party there'd been an accident and a young girl had fallen down the steps. A few eyes turned the way of my friends and I, but our fathers moved onto them in a flash and paid for their enduring silence.

Hell, we even paid off that poor girl's parents, to accept it was just an accident and not to push matters any further. You could say bribery has been a family tradition ever since.

When your friend's reporter mother came snooping around investigating that night, it was easier to nip it in the bud with a cheque, before she found anything more about the story.

Did I know I was sentencing Kimberly Drakeford to death by paying her off? It breaks my heart to say I knew full well what I was doing to that family. I've tried to make it up to them in other ways since, which one day very soon you'll find out about."

Royston watched the tears fall from his son's eyes.

"Why didn't you ever say anything?" the boy sobbed.

"I was eighteen at the time, things were different then. Capital punishment was still a thing, and I was of hanging age. And, believe me, if word got out to the wrong people that I'd killed a disabled girl, accidental or not, I'd have swung for it.

As time went on and people who were paid off started to meet their untimely end, stories began to get whispered about a girl with a porcelain mask visiting them. We hadn't become responsible for just one death anymore; every new death was our burden to bear. With each new body Mr Fisher, and then, my dear Sol, had to bury, it became harder to speak of what happened. The truth had turned to quicksand. The more we struggled with it, the harder it was to find our way out."

Royston looked at the Filofax in his hand and proceeded to make his way to the fireplace where he cast it upon the flames, despite his son's protests.

"It's for the best Willard. No one else needs to yield her wrath."

Willard dried his eyes with his sleeve and smiled a defiant smile at his father.

"You're right, maybe, it is for the best."

Willard said no more, he simply left the room and his father, alone.

A familiar sound then filled the sitting room. It was the sound of the girl with the porcelain face's cries. They would continue without pause for the remainder of the night.

# OCTOBER 31, 1985

# 1

Royston was surprised to see his son at his place at the dining table for breakfast the following morning. No conversation was forthcoming from him though. Usual service had been resumed.

This occasion, however, Royston wanted it to be different. He didn't know how many more chances, if any at all, he would have to tell his son of how proud he was of the person he had become.

He drew a deep breath to prepare for the speech he had prepared in his mind, when he was suddenly thwarted by the sound of the telephone ringing.

He forced himself up from his chair and made his way over to answer it.

"Royston Jennings," he spoke.

"You monster, you deserve to burn in hell," the unidentified female voice spoke from the other line. He hung up the phone and turned his gaze to Willard, who had a satisfied look upon him.

"What have you done?" his father asked.

The phone rang again.

Royston picked up the receiver, expecting another verbal barrage. It came as predicted, this time though, the voice was different.

"Murdering bastard," a man berated.

The phone continued in its relentless ringing after he had hung up. Only this time he chose not to answer. He even went as far as to disconnect it.

"What did you do?" he asked again. Only this time with anger.

"What should have happened a long time ago," the cold answer came.

The phone rang once more, yet there was no way it could have done so. The chord was clearly disconnected.

Royston picked up the handset and was greeted by the taunting sound of multiple voices in a choir of suffering. A number of them were only too familiar. His father, Constance, and Sol included. The sound of Precious's mischievous giggle overlayed all of them.

Royston picked up the phone and threw it hard against the dining room wall.

"Mr Jennings!" a panting voice could be heard from the doorway of the dining room. It was Mrs Weyland. She hadn't been due here this day.

Her face was flushed and had the look about her which suggested she had made her way up to her employer's abode with far more haste and energy than should have been expected of a woman at her age, in her trembling hand she held a piece of paper. It looked to be a page of the Bleddington Gazette. "Tell me this isn't true."

Royston didn't answer, he instead made a beeline for his daily newspaper on the table. He had yet to open it.

He threw a look of contempt to Willard as he flicked through the pages. Then he saw it, tucked in between. A replica cover of the Bleddington Gazette with today's date, stared at him mockingly. The black and white picture of Precious Harper taken the day of her death adorned the page. Above it, the headline read.

**The Death of Precious Harper - Accident or More?**
**An investigation by Kimberly Drakeford.**

The report was the printed text version of the notepad taken from the Filofax. Not a single word had been altered.

# 2

The evening before, around the same time his father was being tormented by his nightmarish visions, Willard had been in the garage of the Drakeford residence with Drake, Tommy, and Finch.

"This is crazy!" Tommy declared as Willard and Drake filled them in on the plan.

"Crazier than being haunted by a vengeful spirit?" Willard's reasoning came.

"But there's got to be over a thousand people living in Bleddington, you expect us to print out a thousand newspapers, we're just school kids, not Rupert bloody Murdoch," Tommy continued.

"We don't need to print out a thousand newspapers," Drake interjected. "We're just printing a one sheet. And we wouldn't need over a thousand. I reckon we'd only need about a few hundred or so. You know how fast word travels in this town, a good scandal like what we're about to give them, would spread like wildfire."

"Finch," Willard contributed. "Do you know the paperboy?"

Finch smiled a mischievous smile of recollection.

"Yeah, I've been known to torment him from time to time, the little shit is scared shitless of me."

"That's good. Well, from our perspective at least, not from his. If he's that scared of you, it will be easier to convince him to add our page into the daily papers as he delivers them tomorrow morning. Tell him that you'll leave him alone in future if he does this for us."

"Do I have to mean it?" Finch quipped.

Willard said nothing, he just threw a stern gaze that only served to elicit a laugh from the bully.

"All we need to do is make the template. Then we just have to work out how to work that printing press," Tommy continued.

The response was matching smiles of satisfaction on the faces of both Drake and Willard.

"What have we missed?" Finch asked.

"It just so happens that we know a certain someone who used to help out on the printing presses when he was younger," Willard confirmed.

Amanda Bakewell's words ran around in his mind once more. 'In a town this size, there's seldom ever any coincidences involved.'

# 3

"Mrs Weyland," Royston spoke with a wavering tone. "You need to take Willard with you and leave this house."

"I don't understand what's going on, Mr Jennings," her frightened reply came.

"Believe me when I say that's a good thing. Thank you, for all you have done for me over the years. Please know that you were never just a cleaner to this house, you were family."

His eyes turned over to his son, he could see the tears starting to well up in his eyes.

"Steady yourself, Willard. We both knew this moment would be coming. I am ready for it. You have given her the truth. I think it's time now that I let her have her revenge."

"It doesn't have to be like this," the boy's defiant response came. "The truth is out now. Maybe that is all she wanted, maybe she can be at peace now, no one else has to die."

"Not the whole truth is out there, son. Mrs Drakeford's story didn't mention what I did to her at the foot of the steps. For her to be at peace, she must fulfil her vengeance, and it ends with me. One more person does have to die."

Willard's tears were freefalling now as his father's words sunk in.

Royston made his way closer to his son.

"I'm proud of you, Willard. I kept a barrier between us so that when this moment came, it would be easier for us. Never once for a moment did it mean that I didn't love you with all of my heart."

The two Jennings' embraced in what had been their first hug since Willard had formed a memory, the reality wasn't lost on either of them that this would also be their last.

"Go on, get out of here," Royston commanded. "I don't want you to see what will happen."

Royston released his grip around the boy and shepherded him towards a sobbing Mrs Weyland. She still had no idea what was going on, but she knew this would be the last time she would see her employer, and more importantly, her friend.

# 4

"I'm ready," Royston shouted from the hall of the manor, once he was sure his son had left the grounds.

His wait wasn't long. As a businessman, he appreciated her promptness, even if her appointment was one of executioner.

The familiar sound of sobbing could be heard from behind him. As loud as the cries were, they had not been enough to overwhelm the cracking sound of bones coming ever closer.

Royston's breaths became more rapid as he attempted, without much success, to calm himself. Despite his legs feeling weaker, he pivoted to face the phantasm. In her hand she held the mask of a grim reaper. It was the mask he had worn that fateful night.

Though it visibly pained the spirit, she handed the mask to Royston and ushered him to put it on.

With her other arm, she reached out to him in a gesture for him to grab her by the crooked, broken hand. Royston complied submissively.

She led him towards the door to Hilltop Manor.

He pondered to himself, if she was in so much pain with every step she took, as she guided him on his walk of death, why wouldn't she just vanish and reappear to the door, as she was capable of?

The sound of cracking bones piercing his ears and making him wince with each sound was answer enough to his internal question. She wanted each anguished step to be a reminder of the pain he and the others had caused her.

They exited the house and took the short walk to the summit of the hill's steps.

It was clear to Royston now what she had intended for him. The most fitting of retributions.

Should he survive the fall, as she had, he would share every piece of agony she had done.

Royston drew a deep breath and held it, in a futile attempt to soften the inevitable pain which would be coming his way.

He felt a hefty blow strike the rear of his rigid, right knee joint forcing him to lose his balance, then the hefty shove came against his back sending him toppling.

He was barely alive as his descent was mercifully stopped by the base of the hill.

The spurts of thick, frothy, plasma he was ejecting from his mouth, struggled to find their way through the breathing hole of the mask, causing him to fight against drowning in his own blood.

He suspected he had punctured a lung and his skull was surely cracked open as he could feel a warm clotting fluid forming a brook beneath his cranium.

He was only able to lift his head high enough to view the barrage of bones sticking out from his torn flesh. His limbs had become skewed to unnatural angles.

Royston struggled to keep his eyes open as his life was oozing from him. His exertions were only rewarded by the pernicious sight of the girl with a porcelain face standing above.

She removed the mask of death from him.

He anticipated her hands clasping around his throat, as he had done to her.

Yet, no such mercy was coming.

She had waited thirty years for her final revenge. She was not going to end it with clemency.

# 5

Police constable, Phil Cummings, found Willard at the home of Mrs Weyland.

It hadn't been his first choice of call after discovering the mangled corpse of Royston Jennings, after the station received an anonymous tip off stating they were concerned for his safety.

After failing to find him at Bleddington Comprehensive, PC Cummings' task of locating the teen had been made easier by the fact the known close associates of the Jennings family, were of an exclusive list.

Having tried the homes of Willard's closest friends, Dominic Drakeford, and Thomas Green, without success, Patricia Weyland had been the next logical stop.

Neither Mrs Weyland, nor Willard appeared surprised by his visit. They had been anticipating it ever since Willard put through the anonymous tip-off.

Though Cummings tried his hardest not to use the word, suicide, when delivering the tragic news to the boy, it was clear this was where his mind was at.

"The damning article which had been placed inside a large number of resident's newspapers this morning, indicting Royston Jennings in the suspected manslaughter of a minor all those years ago must have caused the guilt and panic to resurface, and he took his own life," the constable's instincts told himself when discovering the broken body.

He hadn't completely dismissed murder out of the equation just yet though.

There were enough people in the town who'd already held a vendetta against Jennings for costing them their livelihood.

If anyone was to make an attempt on his life, however, surely, they would have done it by now.

"Have you got somewhere to stay until more permanent plans have been decided upon?" Cummings inquired.

The tragedy of the question was not lost on him this was the second time inside a week he'd had to ask this to a minor following their sole-parent's death, and this time was no easier than the dress rehearsal.

His gaze was aimed as much towards Mrs Weyland as it was for Willard.

"He can stay here for the night, and as long as he wants to after that," Mrs Weyland's immediate answer came. "He's family, after all."

# NOVEMBER 1, 1985

# 1

Willard wasn't surprised to see Drake at Mrs Weyland's door the following morning. He had called his friend to let him know the news the evening before.

Who he was surprised to see, however, was Clifford Drakeford, stood at his son's side looking uncharacteristically nervous.

Willard could tell by the contrasting, unrestrained and excitable expression upon his friend's face that something was afoot, and he was sure he wouldn't have to wait long to find out.

"Can we come in, Mrs Weyland?" Mr Drakeford asked with his customary warmth.

"Of course."

Once seated, Clifford wasted little time in getting to the business of their visit.

"May I begin by saying how sorry I am about your father. The loss of a loved one is never an easy time, believe me, I know. Any time, you ever need someone to talk to, we will both be here for you, without question or hesitation. Which, I guess, leads me as to why I'm here.

This is probably going to be as strange for me to say as it will be for you to hear. I mean, your father and I have only ever had a handful of interactions in the past, which for a town as small as this, is quite an achievement in itself I'd say.

One of those interactions came around nine years ago. Royston turned up unexpectedly at my door one night with a briefcase in hand. He told me he was forever indebted to my wife, and he owed our family more than we could ever envisage.

I had no idea what he had meant. Such was my grieving, I didn't think to press him on the matter. It's something I've thought about on regular occasion since though.

Dominic showed me, this morning, the letter you'd found in the Filofax, and so many questions were answered. When he said he owed us so much, I didn't realise it was Kimberly's life.

Anyways, once your father and I were sat in the living room, he pulled open that beast of a briefcase, that's when he dropped the revelation on me.

Upon his death, I was to become custodian of Hilltop Manor, until his son was of age. Not just the custodian of the house, however. He also asked if I was willing to be the legal guardian of his son too. You, Willard.

He told me that he had heard about what an excellent job I was doing raising Dom since his mother's death, and that he'd heard his son and he were also becoming great friends. He also told me the nobility of a man doesn't come through riches, it comes through adversity, and that I was the most noble man he could think of to ensure his son would become the man he hoped he would have the chance to be.

There was no hesitation on my part. Of course, I would be willing to be your guardian. Honoured, in fact.

As I've watched you grow up to be the person you've become, as tragic as the circumstances are, it truly is my privilege to welcome you to our family. If you'd have us of course.

Willard wept as he embraced Drake and Clifford. The words his father had said to him the night before re-emerged in his mind.

"I've tried to make it up in other ways that one day very soon you'll find out about."

Upon leaving Mrs Weyland's home, Drake playfully punched Willard in the arm, whilst joking over how he was going to get the bigger bedroom in Hilltop Manor now, since Drake was older by a few months, which made him big brother.

He then spoke a more serious sentence which, although short, still said so many words.

"So, the girl with the porcelain face can finally rest now."

"Not yet," the answer came after a brief while of reflection. "There is one more thing I need to do for her."

# 2

Willard pressed play on the cassette deck of the hi-fi system he had taken into the hall of Hilltop Manor.

The sound of Dance Hall Days, by Wang Chung, filled the air.

A part of him felt stupid for even attempting what he had planned in his mind. He had given Precious her justice, now he wanted to give her the happily ever after she'd always dreamed of when she was alive.

He had tried his best to make the hall look like a ball room. Drake, Tommy and even Finch had spent the day helping him decorate it. He made sure he was dressed the part in his charcoal suit he'd had hanging in the back of the wardrobe, after only ever been worn once. Not exactly Prince Charming, but not too shabby, even by his own admission.

Just like the previous Halloween parties at Hilltop Manor, this particular event was by invite only. Unlike those parties, however, there was only to be one person invited by the host. The princess of the ball.

A minute into the song had passed and he was starting to think that his idea may have been folly. Maybe her retribution had been enough to be at rest after all.

The thoughts of turning the cassette off ran through his head, but he saw no point in following through. The efforts of going over to turn off the cassette mid-track were more than just letting it simply finish - and if she wasn't to show, well, at least no one could lay claim to seeing him bust out a few embarrassing moves on the makeshift dancefloor.

The chorus hit, and he felt a presence behind him. Unlike before, however, the temperature of the room didn't drop. It was filled with a reassuring warmth.

"I've been expecting you," he spoke with affection, turning around to face the spirit.

He gave Precious a ceremonial bow before offering his hand to her.

"It's so nice to finally see your face," he continued with sincerity.

She was still dressed in her red, winter coat and yellow wellington boots, but she no longer bore the burden of the cracked porcelain mask.

Her broad smile was infectious. Just as Mr Kready had stated with authority, it was the most enchanting anyone could ever wish to see.

Willard found himself involuntarily grinning helplessly in return.

She moved towards him unrestrained.

There was no painful sobbing now, no hindered movements shackled by her broken body. She took his hand, and they began to dance.

As the outro to the song began and the fade-out commenced, Willard felt a gentle kiss upon his cheek.

Then, the spirit was gone.

She would never be seen again.

# THE END

# ABOUT THE AUTHOR

Steve McElhenny is Welsh, short, and hairy.